MW01672265

THE TOWER

C. R. BUCHANAN
JOHN LEWIS

The Tower is a work of fiction. Any names, characters, business, events, incidents, and anything else in this work of fiction are products of the author/s imagination. Any resemblance to actual persons, living, dead, or soon to be born, is purely coincidental.

Paperback ISBN: 978-1-7366802-2-3
Ebook ISBN: 978-1-7366802-3-0

John Lewis
JLE Cinema Group

www.crbuchanan.com

Editor: Lauren Humphries-Brooks

Lauren Humphries-Brooks is a freelance editor, writer, and film critic with a Master's degree in Cinema Studies from New York University and Creative Writing from the University of Edinburgh. She's the co-host of the feminist film podcast *Citizen Dame,* and has published extensively on The Avengers TV show, Classical Hollywood, and British horror films.

Special thanks:

"Special thanks to my inspiration and the best son a father could ever wish for, Elias Lewis. You are my WHY, my everything."

"And to my mother, Carole, thank you for always being there. I love and appreciate you very much."

"A very special thank you to the person to whom without, none of this would've been possible, Innovative Artists' Melissa Hirschenson…my forever friend, anchor, and center."

"Jeff Bowler, thank you. You've been a true friend throughout the many years and have taught me so much."

—John Lewis

"Trang Nguyễn, thank you for being who you are, showing so much support, and for being a major piece to the puzzle in getting this novel onto the playing field."

"Jeffrey Flexer, you are a continued asset in my development as a writer, and I sincerely thank you for your honesty as a prereader."

"Tearlach Bigger, again, thank you for putting your eyes on this before it went into typesetting and bringing something valuable to light."

"Jason Diamond, thank you for giving this a look at the last minute after my final pass, for being a friend…and for taking an interstellar flight with me to the nearest WolfStar."

"To my family—all of what little I have—my heart is in your hands as usual. Thank you for loving me and giving me strength to do everything I do."

—C. R. Buchanan

Story by John Lewis…

THE TOWER

FOREWORD

"In this story about fluctuating human power and identity, brotherhood and family love, and loyalty and betrayal, John Lewis's agile storytelling brings together a world of fast-paced action and martial arts, peppered with charming, funny moments that will keep you turning pages.

Told through the eyes of Archer Kemp, a hardened military man whose blunt, at times cynical, gaze brings us through warzones, captivity, stolen tender moments, and the interior mental landscapes of his own loss, Lewis's atmospheric descriptions paired with C. R. Buchanan's styling give us the impression of a cinematic experience while reading. He captures the camaraderie of fighters thrust into circumstances beyond their understanding and nimbly guides these characters as they adapt to overcome unexpected horrors.

This is above all an action story, but it gives a solid nod to science fiction with scenarios that raise age-old questions of what it means to be human and what it means when people are forced outside of humanity by a ruthless system.

If you are looking for an action-packed, visually descriptive story about fighting through brutal situations against the backdrop of love, deception, and the strength of tested friendships, then this is the book for you.

Andrzej Bartkowiak 6/27/2021
Andrzej Bartkowiak
~:Filmmaker:~

CHAPTER 1

WAR STORIES

IT IS PEACEFUL in war the moment before you are attacked. No enemy can take that from you. The closest they can come is killing you, but death casts you further into peace. Though I sat beneath beautiful clouds glowing shades of yellow, orange, and red—pierced only by the sun—I long suffered for either that day.

I could see it in my head like a slow-motion angel of death tossed from the heavens above. It was spinning slowly in the reflection of an incoming sunrise amidst the blue. Beige sand hills of vast desert mirrored its deadly elegance with contrasting shade and sunlight as it fell from the sky.

Few understand the beauty of a falling artillery shell.

Its blast shook Earth when it reached its destination and released a payload upon a small group of unsuspecting Taliban soldiers. Dust and debris had no time to settle before battle ensued.

Peace is fleeting.

A dozen Special Forces operators, squad mates of mine, took to shredding through the remaining Taliban. They were methodical and precise, but it was not perfect. The enemy was sneaky. Dirty as war is meant to be.

We thought we had everything covered: angles of attack, the ins, outs, and a solid suppressive game plan, but that was not the case. Slits they had carved into the walls, murder holes as we called them, were hidden in shadows obscured behind hanging pots housing dying plants. We knew not of their presence. Not at first.

Nor could we have known cold steel barrels were looming behind them. Shots that ring out, the ones you are not expecting, those are the ones that get you. Such are the dangers of war.

The enemy shouted as compact, short-barreled, type-56 assault rifles with folding stocks released minor concussions into the air. We did not have to speak Pashto to know what they were saying. Gunshots sound the same in every language.

Two of my squad mates went down immediately as bullets found their marks on legs and torsos. The rest of us sought cover, but that covering was sparse at best. We were pinned.

"Sergeant Kemp," one of my men shouted. "SBB locked and loaded."

He was in position. I scanned to make sure he could

pop his head up for a second without getting it blown off. Enemy gunfire focused on me, and I dropped back down, knowing he was clear to fire.

"Let it loose," I ordered.

The SBB is a Scalable/Selectable Breaching apparatus designed to take shit out. They tell you it is for walls and structural reinforcements, but you can get creative with it. Hell, I have seen what it can do to something as pliable as the human body, but we were breaching a wall that day.

"Fire in the hole," shouted the soldier.

It travels fast when you fire it. You cannot see it, not at that range. Things in front of you just explode. You do not wait for someone to fire the SSB. You wait for the boom.

Earth shook beneath our feet again. A small shockwave hit us. I used the explosion to move for better cover, but the air churned to a blinding state after the detonation. Fragmented concrete, dirt, and dust became airborne around us. It filled our eyes with pain, ears with ringing sensations, and lungs with an unwelcoming mixture to induce coughing.

The soil was desert dry in the barren region of nature's misery we were fighting in but thicker with sediment than we had anticipated. The air churned heavy with it. I tried not to breathe. I tried.

Coughing on both sides of the battlefield accompanied a drop in arms fire. None of us could see. We were all in the same cloud.

Gunshots rang back up as Taliban fired recklessly

through the plume—a spray and pray tactic reserved for the desperate. Sometimes they get lucky and hit their mark. Most of the time, it is nothing more than a waste of ammo.

I ducked and moved while feeling blindly for cover. My boots slipped in silt, and I fell, crawling around a corner and stirring up more dust to mix with the debris. I needed cover. The sense of touch and sound alone guided me blindly until I felt something: hard rubber bumps, metal bolts, a rim. It was the tire on that beat-up, piece of shit, broke-down ass truck outside the enemy stronghold.

I needed to see. There was no way to kill the son-of-a-bitches until I could. I thought about lobbing a grenade over the rusted truck, but I was unsure who I would hit.

On another note, canteens are more than something to drink from. I reached for mine and laid on my back to avoid getting shot with a lucky-ass bullet. Its lid was tight. I had to wipe the dust from my hands onto my undershirt to unscrew it.

A painful scratching sensation filled my eyes as I tilted them towards a once blue sky and washed them out. They were nearly clean when a bullet of unknown origin kissed sharply into my left rib.

"Ah…" I shouted. "Motherfuckers."

I held position behind the rusty truck. It came into view with clearing eyes under settling debris; then I pulled up my jacket and shirt to find out how badly I had been hit: a hole in my uniform, a tear on my flesh. It was a burning graze and nowhere near as bad as I thought it would be, but rusted trucks make for piss-poor covering. I was unable to move without getting shot again.

Captain Sheppard signaled a clear message from behind a military Humvee fortunate enough not to be hit with a grenade or RPG yet: his pointer finger to him, ridge side of his left hand to his temple, pointer finger back to me, then his palm went back down and lowered towards the Earth. The man was about to lay down suppressive fire, and I was to relocate.

He volleyed lead, I moved behind a small concrete reinforcement, and he retook cover, all but saving my life. But we were far from being out of the situation.

The dust settled, and our enemies became transparent behind a vast hole the SBB had been so charitable to create. It was payback time for the fallen, and I would be damned if someone were going to beat me to the front of the line.

"SBB breach successful," Captain Shepard's voice filled the air. "Thunder-flash and advance. I'll lay cover. Find Mujahid."

"Roger that," I said.

The M84 stun grenade—something I had a secret affinity for—came off my fatigues, and I tossed it into the breached wall of the enemy compound. The pop was loud. A flash surged from the SBB formed cavity and murder holes in unison like a shattering sun to light the dustbowl around us.

Captain Shepherd laid fire. "Go. Go. Go."

I rushed towards the enemy compound in heavy gear light-footed under controlled adrenaline and entered the enemy stronghold.

1-2
THE HARD PUSH

RAT-TAT-TAT-TAT.

A few short bursts separated a pair of enemies' brains from their encasements. Fuck it. Two less to worry about.

I pushed through the weakened structure as the enemy called out to one another, to us maybe. No fucking clue what they were saying. They were screaming some serious shit, but their intentions nor desires mattered to me. A few more steps and another M84 were about to bless me with the luxury of shooting the blind. Its pop told me to move.

RAT-TAT-TAT-TAT.

I shot all three. Two died instantly, but one was stubborn, and I was left alone to deal with him as my squad mates cleared the remaining Taliban from the camp.

It was time to handle the situation or die. Other options are Hollywood fairytales that do not exist in actual warfare. I kicked a long-barreled rifle away from the final enemy and knocked him back with a sharp blow to his forehead, staying alert to my surroundings as he gurgled babble through a nasty chest wound.

"Where's Hafiz Mujahid?" I asked.

He moaned but offered no information. He needed help speaking, something I gladly obliged him with as I placed the heel of my boot on his wound. I have always been a generous man like that.

"Where's Hafiz Mujahid?" I repeated.

He pointed down a nearby hallway.

TΛT.

One less to suffer.

1-3
WOMEN AND CHILDREN

I moved cautiously through a battered, makeshift hallway. Concrete walls within it were old and cracked. A bucket of fly-laced feces released a disgusting odor in which the enemy was immune. It felt like a reaper's haven for all those who dared enter, and it was a perfect place to find that peace I had been seeking. I entered wishing his scythe sharp, swift, and with my name etched into it should he see me.

A door at the other end of the makeshift hall held harbor to whimpering women and children. I would not kill them, not unless I had to, but my eagerness needed settling before entering. I paused my trigger finger long enough to relax and squeeze instincts tightly to my chest before cracking the door.

I moved a small mirror from my pocket to check the room. A woman and several children came into view. They were scared and possibly strapped with C4. I could not take chances. I eased the mirror back into my pocket, slid open the door, and turned through its threshold with heightened caution.

"Hafiz Mujahid?" I asked.

The woman and children did not say anything. I could not hold it against them. To answer me directly would have been a death sentence for their loved ones. The woman caring for the kids moved a few feet to her side to shed light on our target. He was sitting behind them in a corner—another foreign coward hiding behind innocence.

"Put your hands where I can see them," I said.

"Compound clear." I adjusted the com on my collar to ensure someone would hear me. "Target acquired."

"Copy that," answered Captain Shepherd.

He must have already been making his way towards us through the compound. Seconds later, he appeared.

"Good job, Master Sergeant," said Captain Shepherd. "Foot back to extraction."

"Sir?" I asked. "Shouldn't I stay and help secure the package?"

"Negative. Head back to extraction. That's an order, Master Sergeant."

"Yes, sir."

Nothing about it felt right. It was a gut feeling. Instincts said not to leave and stayed with me as I made my exit. I almost stopped twice to go back but chose to follow Sergeant Shepherd's orders. The military had us programmed to obey.

1-4
UNLAWFUL SHOTS

Heavy thoughts regarding my instincts popped up as I moved back through the wounded compound and made my exit into a scorching sun. Not long would pass before I heard it: the physical struggle, feet sliding on sandy concrete potted with bare spots of earth, a screaming woman, and crying children.

"Back off," shouted Captain Shepherd from within the compound. "I said back off. Now."

I tried to ignore it, silence it in my head, and keep moving, but screams from women and children are hard to bear even in war.

RAT-TAT-TAT-TAT.

More screams.

RAT-TAT-TAT-TAT-TAT-TAT.

My head whipped. I tore back into the compound as the helpless cried out.

RAT-TAT-TAT-TAT.

CHAPTER 2

CHRISTY

BITCH—THE SONG FROM the Rolling Stones—oddly matched the gunfire as I woke. My eyes adjusted. A framed picture of a younger me in that damn military uniform came into view.

"Fucking alarm."

I was groggy. It was late, and I silenced the call long enough to lay my head back down before the phone rang again. I was not going to answer it until I fucked up and looked at it:

'THE BITCH…'

It was my ex-wife. She had earned the name, but I needed to answer, nonetheless. I was sure it was about my son. It was always about him or money when she called.

I pressed the answer key. "Hey. What's up?"

"Christopher didn't come home again," answered Christy.

"What time is it?"

"Eleven, I think. Eleven fifteen."

My head was killing me from dehydration. I barely ate half the time and had not drunk anything in a day, not unless you count Bulliet Rye Whiskey. It is lackluster in its ability to hydrate but an easy way to forget about the world's stress looming over you if you pound enough shots and give it time to take effect.

"He's thirteen years old, Christy," I said. "What's the point of having full custody if you can't handle him? This is the kind of stuff that wouldn't happen if he were with me."

"No," she said. "You're right. He'd just be hungry all the time."

"What the hell's that supposed to mean?"

"It means I don't need your bullshit right now, Archer. Can you just find your son? Please?"

"As always." I ended the call.

She had cheated on me with someone I was close to years ago and left me feeling I never wanted to waste my time looking for anyone else. Part of me thought I was too fucked in the head with PTSD. Part of me could care otherwise.

I did not need her. I needed almost no one. My son, Christopher, was the only person I required approval from to keep living.

I moved into the kitchen with the usual lousy

attitude after talking with her. Food and water were necessary before I puked all over myself and ruined the clothes I was still wearing from the day before.

2-2
NURSING A HANGOVER

I guess she was right. The fridge was always empty. I was not much of an eater. You could say I was going through some shit, but that was something for me to deal with when I got around to it.

Thirsty thoughts guided me to the sink. My throat was parched. It was sore from last night's suffering under self-induced misery and thoughts about ending my existence. That sometimes happened if I drank too much, which was more sometimes than others.

Everyone thought I would probably bring Brad Paisley and Alison Krauss's "Whiskey Lullaby" anthem to life one day—put that bottle of whiskey to my head and pull the trigger—minus the goodbye note. They did not know me. No one did. Sure, I had thought about suicide more than once over the hundred or so days before that night, but I could not leave that weakness to be the final message to my son.

I would accept peace if it came, but it would not be from my hands.

I pounded one glass of water, then a second and a third before I stopped and stuffed my face with leftover

Chinese food. It was glazed with a thin goo and would most likely make me sick, but nothing else was available to eat. I could have used a good puking but should have been writing dates on stuff.

I finished my plate and stacked it into the sink amongst a mountain of other dishes. I was not lazy. I simply held no yearning to wash them. I needed a maid or something. A personal assistant?

I headed back into my bedroom to get dressed in an old warn-out hoodie. It was a favorite of mine. Old jeans that matched it went on before I took to the streets.

CHAPTER 3

SEARCHING FOR BLOOD

SIDEWALKS, WHERE I was searching for Christopher, were dirtier than a seventy-year-old pedophile. It was not just bubble gum and cigarette butts either. It was a neighborhood littered with waste. An empty bag tumbled by and snuggled itself around my shin as I walked, but I did not bother to deal with it. No fucks given. I kept walking.

My pace slowed as I passed a dark collection of unsavory characters in the low-income neighborhood. Lights flickered unkept by a city holding no qualms for starving the poor. It was scum's haven and only six blocks from where I called home.

My nose wrinkled. The scent of urine struggled to match its surrounding filth. I could not stand it. It pissed me off, but I had to keep looking for my son. He was all I barely had.

The whole neighborhood was a visual letdown: a burning barrel of fire underscored a man shooting heroin in plain sight, scantily dressed hookers leaned into car windows, johns talked with them in flirtatious tones as if they actually cared about the bitches, and trash bled down the street with every puff of polluted night air. It led me to the same question every time I walked those streets in the dead of night. A question of hopeful desire: why can't diseases in humans be deadlier and spread faster?

I walked beyond the corners of three more damaged buildings. A more dangerous part of the neighborhood was coming up ahead, one I never had to enter to reach my destinations. Though he had not found me over the years, I often walked past those streets wondering if my maker was hiding somewhere in obscurities.

Years had passed since the war, yet part of me was still looking for peace. Internally? Externally? I could not say, but some aspirations never leave a man—not when they are strong enough to run a fragment of his natural life.

A group of young men with tatted necks and faces were selling Fentanyl to an addict on the corner ahead, but my son was not with them. I paused to watch them for a moment, wasting time before moving on. They were nobodies, they would die nobodies, and nobody would miss them.

The other side of the street and its nearby blocks were held nightly hostage by a few alleyways that ran between them. They were treacherous, occupied by the deepest lowlifes and bottom-feeders visiting the neighborhood—ones with blades and guns as improper tools for exchanges destined to be one-sided.

There were several people down it, but I could not tell if my son was amongst them. I studied the scene. Backlighting from a weak streetlight cast their faces to be nothing more than silhouettes.

I put my head down, leaving my nose and mouth only partially exposed under the warn-out hoodie as my pace slowed. The alleyway was known for trouble and the worst one he could have been hanging out in, especially at night.

"Christopher better not have his ass down there," I mumbled.

I took a few steps in for a better view. A group of degenerate thugs was clustering around someone. I watched for a moment, curious if one of the boys were my son or not, before sliding the hoodie off my head and entering.

3-2
DEALERS

I approached gradually under a vale of darkness, hidden by an old, red brick, earth-carpeted alleyway keen on sheltering secrets. They were selling drugs to a couple of teenagers, none of which looked old enough to smoke or as if their futures contained anything promising.

It was not the kind of place one wants to walk in hopes of finding his son, but some kids have problems. Mine was one of them. I scanned the group, but the dealers were doing their thing without him.

I watched on for a moment before turning to continue my search through the streets. The punks were whispering behind me. A few steps later, I heard footsteps.

“Hey, you,” called the first drug dealer.

I stopped. I should not have.

“You lost?” the dealer continued. “You must be.”

I turned to face them. I was honest in my answer, though he was incapable of reading its underlining.

“Yeah,” I answered. “I am lost.”

“Give me your wallet,” said the dealer, “and I’ll point you in the right direction.”

“You guys know a kid named Christopher?”

“Are you deaf, Grandpa?”

“He’s thirteen.” I held my hand up with my palm down. “About yay tall.”

"Old man." The dealer shook his head. "I'm trying to be nice here, but hand it over, or you're dead."

I thought about killing him. I thought about killing them all. I thought about walking away.

A thousand unnoticed ideas bordering on subliminal impulses probably ran through my head, none of which they would like. Maybe this was it? Perhaps the reaper was on the lurk after all? Peace could have been waiting for me in the next few minutes, and I was willing to stick around and find out.

"Why don't you give me your wallet?" I asked. "Give me all your wallets."

The hilarious expression on his face as he looked at the others: shocked, stupid, confused. I doubt he often received feedback, not the way I had just given it to him. Not from a stranger. He turned back to me, thinking he knew how things were about to go down.

Neither of us feared death, but only one of us hoped for it from time to time.

"Guy's a comedian." The dealer pulled a knife from his pocket. "What'd you say again?"

He stopped talking after that. I guess that is what happens when someone smacks you in the esophagus with a tightly closed fist. At least that has been my experience.

I watched him as he dropped to his knees. I held no feelings about it. I simply watched, praying one of the others had a gun. I was hoping more so they knew how to use it. Yeah, I was having one of those nights, but it did not take long to find out.

The second dealer rushed me and pulled a handgun from the back of his Dickies, signaling he had no idea what the fuck he was doing. He was too close when he raised it to fire. His arm either fractured or broke. I have no idea. I am not a doctor. I just remember the pop.

I dismantled his gun and dropped it to the ground one component at a time like a jigsaw puzzle with a piece missing—because I kept the barrel. The weight of the cold steel felt good in my pocket. Then I stomped his chest a bit more than I probably should have.

The teenagers buying from the froth took off. It was a wise decision. Sticking around could have left them rocking dentures from wheelchairs for the rest of their lives with bags on their hips to shit through.

The rest of them rushed, but I had something they could not see. It was internal, and the unholy can of whoop-ass I handed them was filled with a special kind of violence far past its expiration date. I had been holding on to it for nearly a decade, and its flavor had gone south.

Vicious shots landed. First, a right under one of the thug's jaw, then a left to another's temple. The aggression released a bit of the pent-up anger trapped in my heart.

Two of the punks' heads cracked against the red brick wall at my right. One of them more than once as the last of the bunch tried to pull me off him. Skinny bastard paid for trying to help. More pops followed once he lost consciousness: shoulders, knees, wrist, elbows, ankles. I broke them all so his shitbag friends could have fun spending the next several months wiping his ass for him.

The first dealer, the punk still clutching his throat like a wounded insect, could barely speak when I moved back to him and rested my foot on the hand he was holding his throat with.

"Stop…" He struggled to speak. "I'm sorry. Please."

Please is a funny-sounding word when it comes from a predator's mouth. It is one of those words they hear all the time and choose to ignore. It is how they live. I thought it best to pay it forward.

"Pick it up," I said.

"Pick up what?" asked the dealer.

"The knife."

"Hell no. We're… We're sorry. We didn't mean anything by it."

Old knees attached to a man too cold to care about the pain bent down so I could reach the knife and extend it to him.

"Ain't no way, bro," the dealer continued. "Keep it."

"Don't call me bro," I said. "You're not my brother."

"The fuck's wrong with you?"

He was scared. He thought I was going to kill him. I thought about it and the lives I had taken in the past. Desire to take another was not fully present. Besides, parenting from prison would have most likely proven itself to be more difficult for me than it already was.

"Now," I said, "give me your wallet."

"I…I don't got one. I swear."

I flipped the knife blade down and plunged it into the ground at his side. It was for show more than anything else, mostly.

"Okay, okay." He handed me a stack of cash rolled and bound with a rubber band. "Chill."

I loomed over him to count it when Christy called again, coaxing me to place the phone on speaker and set it on the delinquent's chest. "Not a fucking word."

"What?" asked the dealer.

I struck him until he was puddled in his dreams, swallowing blood and teeth as he slept. He was willfully dense, something that drove me into bedlamite.

"What was that?" asked Christy.

"Nothing." I finished counting the cash. "What's up?"

"Okay…" She paused, knowing I was lying. "Well, sorry to bug you, but Christopher's back."

"Okay. Tell him I'll call him tomorrow."

"Sure. Bye." She hung up.

I grabbed my phone before pulling the hoodie back over my head and walking from the alleyway, leaving the insect alone with his dreams.

CHAPTER 4

THE HOMELESS VET

THE WALK HOME felt lonelier than usual. I needed something to distract my thoughts. Thankfully, I was not the only war vet on the streets that night. There was another less fortunate than me.

A homeless man sitting against a nearby wall came into sight. I knew he would be around there somewhere, and I had often seen him posted up next to makeshift tents and cardboard boxes. We never spoke until that night.

He was missing both his legs and dressed in raggedy military fatigues. A lot of homeless dressed the part for extra handouts. I had no idea if he was the type or not. Seeing how I had some extra cash on me, I figured it was time to stop and find out.

"You served?" I asked.

"Yes, sir," he answered. "Iraq. Third Division in combat, third Battalion to flow in under Desert Storm."

"Ahh." I snickered. "You boys didn't mess around. Talil Airfield, Najaf."

"No, sir. I only got to do two tours, though. C4 made sure of that. You?"

"What makes you think I served?"

"You knew about Talil Airfield, didn't you?" he answered. "I would've known anyhow. I can see it in your eyes."

"Yeah," I said. "O.D.A. Master Sergeant."

The man sat upright to salute. I am positive he would have stood had it not been for missing both his legs and being without a wheelchair, but he was still proud. He was still saluting.

"Master Sergeant," he said, "it's an honor."

Catching me smiling is hard to do. It hurts my cheeks, but he brought it out of me when extending his hand for a shake that night. I did not shake it, but the Third Battalion tattoo on his forearm next to what looked like an entry wound from a 7.62×39mm round the AK-47 rifle fires—loved by the Taliban in the region he claimed to have served—confirmed he was the real deal.

I placed the wad of cash I took from the filth a few streets over into his hand. "Stay proud, brother."

The stack of cash I handed him was thickly rolled with hundreds, no doubt a few thousand dollars. I never finished counting it, and the homeless veteran did not rifle through it before I left.

His face lit up like a six-year-old at his first surprise party. "Thank you. Thank you, Master Sergeant."

It was nice. Tranquility is sometimes a gift only a night sky can give you, but its blessing belonged to him. He had sacrificed more than I had for the country and deserved it.

I made it to the sidewalk across from my apartment's front door. A pair of uniformed officers were standing over a man across the street and caught my attention. He was handcuffed and sitting on the curb. Red and blue lights flashed in ovulating rhythm over a silent patrol car. I watched them spin until the reflecting lights sent me to another time—Red and blue like the ice cream parlor.

4-2
PEANUT BUTTER ICE CREAM

The ice cream parlor's lights circled next to an old, barbershop-style candy cane spin above an order window. I was sitting next to Christopher back when he was only ten years old. Those were the good days.

We were tearing into a pair of tall ice cream cones. We dripped sweat, and the heat forced us to keep up with a runaway melting process making our hands messy.

"I thought you liked peanut butter," I said.

"I do," answered Christopher. "Not on ice cream, though."

"Have you tried it?"

"No." Christopher licked drippings from his hand and the edge of the cone. "Don't have to."

I tried passing him my cone for a taste, but he would not take it. He was stubborn—no idea who he could have gotten it from.

"Buddy," I said. "If you try something and you don't like it, that's one thing, but you can't say you don't like something if you've never tried it. Well, at least not when it comes to food and ice cream."

His face wrinkled. "But peanut butter and ice cream?"

"Yes." I laughed. "Peanut butter and ice cream."

He shook his head and made another squinty face.

"Just try it," I urged. "Best thing since sliced bread."

"They sponsor you or what?" asked Christopher. "Geez...frickin' peer pressure."

"Hey." I cut him the daddy-look. "Language."

"But frick isn't a bad word."

"It is if I say it is."

"What?" He shook his head. "That's not how it works."

I could not keep myself from laughing. He was technically correct, and I was not about to argue his logic.

"Okay," I said. "What if I give you something? A trade for your bite. Would you try it then?"

"Dad, you're acting obsessed." He paused to think about it for a second. "Give me what?"

He had always been a curious kid. I pulled something from my pocket to entice him, something I had carried through wars over the years for good luck. I held it up proud and ready to impress him.

"A nickel?" he asked. "What do I look like? I'm not five."

"But this is no ordinary nickel," I said. "Look at it. Seriously."

He took it from me and rotated it in his fingers to examine both sides.

"See," I continued. "There's a buffalo on one side and an Indian on the other. It's called a buffalo nickel."

"Looks like a regular old nickel to me," he said.

"It isn't, but you're right about the old part. It's from a long time ago. See the stamp? Nineteen twenty-six. I'll bet it is worth a small grip over what it used to be."

"Really? Like how much?"

"I don't know. A couple of bucks, maybe fifty for all I know."

"Fine," he said. "Just one bite?"

"Just one bite."

I had him, which was not always an easy thing to accomplish with Christopher. He took a bite and smiled. I felt like I had won a small battle until he handed me his cone and refused to give mine back.

4-3
STREETLIGHTS

My smile faded when the squad car doors slammed shut and brought me back to the real world. The officers turned off the lights and departed with their captive. They pulled away to leave me staring alone into an empty street.

Flickering streetlights alternating darkness and light reflected my life the months preceding that night. I would usually feel fine one minute—as if there were a light at the end of the tunnel I had walked so long. The next day I might feel like firing a round-up my right nostril. Not cocaine, though. I shied away from drugs.

There is irony in not wanting to take something that could seriously harm your body and drinking as much as I did, but whiskey was a far cry from cocaine or a bullet. I had thought about both, but I was not that weak. I think everyone has thought about mortality at some point.

I swallowed the notion and dismissed it all together before calling Christopher for a fatherly lecture. It rang, and rang, and rang. Then it stopped.

"Hello?" he asked.

"Hey, buddy," I said. "Where you at?"

"Hello?"

"Hello." I checked my reception. "Can you hear me?"

"Can you hear me?" he asked.

"Yeah. Where are—"

"Ha, ha. Leave a message, and I'll get back with you."

His recording beeped.

"Very funny. Got me again, punk. Talked to your mom. We were getting worried about you. Love you. Bye, bye." I almost hung up and brought it back to my ear at the last second. "But I better hear from you soon. I'm not joking. Bye."

He had gotten me with that old prank voicemail so many times I could not remember anymore. He was good at it and changed his recordings every week or less, making it impossible not to get fooled by new ones.

I moved up the front steps to my apartment and unlocked the door, taking one last look to imagine my son walking towards my house with me, but he was not. He never was. The only times I saw him were the court scheduled times that I picked him up.

CHAPTER 5

ABDUCTION

I DID SOMETHING FOR the first time in months when I entered my apartment. I locked the deadbolt—no idea why. I just did.

My apartment was a shithole. It matched the surrounding neighborhood and my personality to the letter. These were rough times.

Dusty memorabilia consisting of medals from grappling tournaments hung from the ceiling above an aged television. A pair of framed photos sitting on top of it encompassed my twelve-man Green Beret team. Next to it was a picture of me, Christopher, and Christy from a time where peace stood fast in our lives. They were all at the living room's center against the wall, and a TV stand further past its prime than me supported it all.

On a stand next to the television sat a picture of

myself and my younger brother, Elias. We were training together for an upcoming fight the day Christy snapped the photo. We were both sweaty and releasing tired smiles. I loved that picture, though it harbored bad memories and turned out to be the last smile we would share. It was also the last picture I would ever watch Christy take in person.

A wall opposite the TV is one I kept adorned with outdated UFC Championship belts and military decorations from the days before I opened my camp. Frankly, that wall was the second-best thing in the apartment, beaten out only by a photo of me holding Christopher in fight shorts when he was a baby.

I would nearly kill to get those days back, but some things are not meant to be. It is better to accept the facts in life and move on. Several minutes passed while I reflected on it before moving to my bathroom.

5-2
NUMBER TWO

It was the biggest shit I had taken in weeks.

I move to exit under the sound of a flushing toilet when something in the mirror caught my attention—my ugly ass face. It was full of bumps, bruises, and scars from old scuffles.

KNOCK-KNOCK-KNOCK.

It did not budge me. Whoever it was, they would knock themselves into boredom and leave if I ignored it.

KNOCK-KNOCK-KNOCK.

It was irritating, and I had no cares for whom it was. I kept picking my face.

KNOCK-KNOCK-KNOCK.

"Damn it to hell."

It was becoming clear they were not going to leave. I had to either answer it or go crazy listening to it. Since I was already going crazy at heart, I chose the former.

5-3
TOUGH GUY

I walked back to the front door, thinking it was a good thing I locked the deadbolt. I had no idea who it was, and nobody wants to defend themselves while taking a shit. Who knocks that much anyway?

I should have used the peephole when I answered the door. I should have always used it. Sure, it was in all likelihood an unwise choice not to use it in a neighborhood like that, but it was subconsciously in my nature those months to challenge my presence on the planet.

I went carelessly for the door handle and opened it. A large, dark-suited man tried to stand tough on the other side of the threshold.

"Can I help you?" I asked.

"Archer Kemp," he answered. "I need you to come with me."

I snickered. "You a cop?"

"Not exactly."

"Detective? FBI? Anyone connected to the state or federal government?"

"No."

"Then maybe you should fuck off before something bad happens to you."

The scoundrel reached into his coat to show me he was packing heat—a Styer M4-A1 9mm pistol—an attempt to intimidate the wrong person. It was a nice sidearm but a bad mistake. A moment later, he was on his hands and knees with a red rush of blood puddling into my carpet. Noses bleed a lot like that when you push them into the back of someone's face.

"Reconsidering fucking off yet?" I asked. "Because you picked the wrong guy today."

Cold steel has a unique feeling when it hits the back of your head. At least it does mine. I felt it that day, right before everything blurred out and my hands met the floor in a failed attempt to catch myself. I knew what had happened. I wanted to stand back up, but my body was betraying me. I was dizzy for just reasons.

"No," said another voice. "You're definitely the right guy."

His voice resonated as my living room disappeared into blackness, leaving me to wonder how the hell he got into my apartment. The tone of his words was a familiar one, but I was too jacked-up from the blow he delivered to place it. I could barely make it out but had no problem processing the fact blood was curving around my cheeks before I lost consciousness.

CHAPTER 6
SHORE LEAVE

A BEAUTIFUL DAY EMBODIED San Diego on the Coronado Municipal Beach during my first military leave in nine years. It was to California, a place I never thought of as pleasant enough to live. Elias and I were sitting in a gazebo. Magic danced in the hearts and eyes of all around us but none more than hers—green and beautiful.

My brother was sipping a Bourbon Old Fashioned and asking how long I planned to continue serving in the armed forces. He was curious to learn if I would continue training, teaching, and fighting when I got out and what our long-term goals together were. But I kept her in the corner of my eye as he talked.

Elias wanted to open a school together, a big one, and it did not seem like a bad idea. I agreed it would be a great thing, but I had to meet this girl. She called to me like a siren stranded on an island's sand far from her salty home.

She looked my way a few times. I was unsure if it was because she noticed me looking at her, was weirded out, or if she was into me until she smiled. That is when I caught her trying to turn fast enough to hide her eyes. Her friend was laughing and kept nudging her shoulder.

"What do you keep looking at?" asked Elias.

"Sorry." I sipped black tea. "Go ahead. I'm listening."

He looked over his shoulder. "Just go talk to her, bro."

"I don't know what you're talking about."

"Come on." He leaned back in his chair to cut me a smartass look. "Like I don't know you or that look in your eyes. Haven't seen that look in about a decade. So, go talk to her."

He was right. It had been a while, and she was more than just pretty. Her black hair dyed with auburn-streaks caught the sun as if to capture and never surrender it. The way she moved… She was a temptress designed for conquest and had my heart rolling before I realized it was heading down a slope leading to love.

"All right." I stared. "Okay."

"For real?" asked Elias. "You're actually going to try and throw some game?"

"Sure." I stood from the table. "Why not?"

Elias pulled out his cell and held it my way.

"What are you doing?" I asked.

"Big, bad, big brother Archer about to try making a move…" he answered. "No way in hell I'm missing this."

"Funny. Put that shit away, man."

"All right." He laughed. "But I'm watching this. I've never seen a train derail in person."

"You can do me better than watching if you want."

"Oh yeah?"

"Yeah." I laughed. "Come be a good wingman for me."

He looked their way again. They glanced our way from time to time, smiling amongst themselves.

"Think her friend's single?" asked Elias.

"You know as much as I do."

"Fuck it." Elias shot the rest of his drink and stood from the table. "You might want to have yourself an Old Fashioned with me before you go over there."

"You know I don't drink."

"Might wish you did in a minute, but whatever… Let's do it."

6-2
ELIAS'S INTRODUCTION

I approached the girls, focusing on the one that enraptured me, and was about to introduce myself when Elias stepped between us.

"Hi," he said. "My brother here has been seriously

stuck on you for the last thirty minutes and didn't have the balls to come talk to you. I'm here to help him out."

My little brother thought he was funny like that, but the girls were laughing. No harm, no foul.

"Thanks, Elias." I turned to face her. "Ignore him. He's the village idiot."

"My name's Christy." She held out her hand for a shake. "This is my friend Julie."

Elias took his time shaking Julie's hand. "And a beautiful friend she is."

She smiled. My little brother was already working his magic, and he was good at it. It is the one thing about him I could never top.

"Archer." I shook Christy's hand like a gentleman in an old black and white movie, then turned to her friend and motioned to my little brother. "This is Elias. He was telling me over there at our gazebo that he likes the way you sip your drink."

"What?" asked Elias. "I'd never say something that corny. Trust me."

The girls looked at one another, giggling, and asked us to sit with them. Elias punched my shoulder as I pulled up a chair to talk with Christy. He did his own thing with her friend, but I was still thinking about the velvet softness of my target's touch and how it lingered in the palm of my hand when I sat.

I told her I was on leave for another month and that I would be back on tour for another six after that. She was not put off by it like I thought she would be. Nor did she use it as an excuse to have a little fun on the side. As far as choices and opportunities go, I would have been okay with either for a shot at getting to know her, but she was keen on the whole military thing. It turns out her father and brother both served.

It was the best first conversation I had ever shared with someone. It was flawless. Effortless. We talked until the early hours, and neither of us wanted it to end.

6-3
TIMELESS MOMENTS

Seven months later, my tour was over. I had sent a hundred letters back and forth with Christy and made dozens of phone calls. My letters to her were filled with the usual. They possessed thoughts of me missing her, wanting to see her again, and needing her in my life—most outlined in poetry.

Her letters to me were similar, minus the poetry. She claimed not to be a poetic person, but something about the way she wrote melted cold regions of my heart. She centered me, and my soul became healthy when she was around.

We had not moved in together, though we had talked about it. We wanted things to be correct, and neither of us was in a rush. I loved her and had no reservations about her love for me.

Christy was in my kitchen cooking breakfast as she

usually did when she stayed over. Bacon and egg-scented air filled my nostrils. I smiled and watched her; everything within me knew she was the one.

She was in my old army shirt. It was two sizes too big for her, but she made it look adorable. I looked her over from head to toe, starting with the hair covering her neckline to drape over her right shoulder. The shirt hung off her left, hiding slender curves beneath it. Toned hamstrings and calves peeked from its bottom to nearly show that perfect little ass of hers. A teasing cloth—that is what she was wearing.

"I'm keeping this shirt," she said. "Just thought you should know that."

I was okay with it. It looked better on my lover anyhow.

"How'd you know I was standing here?" I asked.

"I can feel you."

"More than last night?"

"Well…" She cut me a smile. "I wouldn't go that far."

She turned off the stove and moved the pans from the heat. Her legs tangled me up to the curves of her darling little backside protruding from beneath the shirt. It was tempting, but I had another plan.

I approached her, kissed her exposed shoulder, and ran my palms down the sides of her hourglass with barely enough contact for her to feel, teasing as I went. Her breathing shifted erotically as I lowered myself behind her to clamp down on her hips. My teeth all but left marks when I bit softly on the inside of her cheeks.

"Oh my..." she exhaled.

I stopped long enough for her to turn in curiosity. She gasped when she saw me on a knee with the little black box open to reveal sparkling diamonds. Her eyes were wide over a hand covering her mouth.

"Christy—" I said.

"Yes," she interrupted with a bit of hop. "Yes, Archer. In a heartbeat, I'll marry you."

I laughed. "You're supposed to wait for me to finish."

"I'm sorry." She wiped tears from her eyes and tried to compose herself. "I'm just..." She went to her tippy-toes and wrapped her arms around my neck. "I don't need the speech, Archer. I love you." She pulled me from the kitchen. "Now come make love to me again."

She knew I was not the best with words and was most likely throwing me a bone. It was one of many reasons I loved her, and I had to marry her. When she kissed me, it was as if she, and she alone, controlled the destiny of the stars.

CHAPTER 7

BARS

MY HAPPY WORLD was gone. A wave of little itches and subtle vibrations moved through me. My body was twitching. Someone shouted into the blackness of my space, but I could not make anything out. I squinted and rubbed my eyes. Nothing helped. My name bounced around in the back of my mind like a subliminal dream attempting to become a reality, but I remained unable to answer the call.

"Archer..." the voice continued.

It became clearer. Someone I knew was shouting for me. It felt like I was still dreaming, but my attention was being beckoned. Desperation filled the voice.

"Yo, Archer. Wake up..."

My lungs filled with a gasp as I woke, and my body jolted. My head was killing me. It pounded as if my brain had an agenda and begged for permission to pursue it. My eyes were adjusting but in no hurry to assist me. Whoever hit me in the back of the head did it with force, but I was steadily coming around. Wherever I was, I was not alone.

Concrete came into view under a matching ceiling. I was on a bed somewhere I should not have been. Nothing made sense. It was warm, almost hot, and sweat burned into the corners of my eyes when I sat up to look around.

It was impossible to concentrate. I rubbed the back of my head: a knot, a lump, and dried blood. A glance at my fingertips revealed them a wet red after I touched it. That is the result of being blindsided with a loaded firearm. They had hit me harder than I thought they had.

"Motherfucker…" I grunted.

I popped my neck to the right and stretched to release tension. It proved to be less helpful than I thought it would, but I took what I could get. I popped it left to relieve more stress and noticed what looked to be jail bars as my eyes struggled to clear themselves.

The mattress had no give when I moved to push myself up. I stopped to remain seated and found less than a bed beneath me—a prison cot and a thin cushion was all that was present to offer relief to an aging back with a lifetime of abuse behind it. Another just like it sat empty at the other end of my cell.

I was trapped in five sides of concrete heavily coated with glossy grey paint and a wall of bars. A square-shaped steel panel with a seam running its center was inset into the ceiling for unknown reasons. It was vaguely familiar, though my last stint with the law offered no freshly painted walls.

A colored cloth, one far from matching the scene, snagged my attention.

"The hell is this?" I asked no one.

I was wearing an orange prison uniform and held captive like a stray dog snagged from the streets with an unknown date to be put down. It was too crazy to be happening, but the partially dried blood on the back of my head coaxed me to accept it.

I stood and walked to the edge of my new cage, dizzy, light-headed, and needing an aspirin the way Charles Manson needed Jesus. The cell moved in ways it should not have. I was swaying off-balanced. I grabbed the bars to stabilize myself.

Cold steel bars pressed into each side of my forehead when I leaned into them. A drop of sweat at the tip of my nose hung in place. A moment passed, and it dripped to the floor. I watched it puddle with disoriented thoughts and turned my eyes forward.

More cells came into focus across a wide walkway separating us. My vision was still a little cloudy, but I could tell its occupants were wearing clothes matching mine. Whether or not I was alone was no longer a question. Misery _____ company. Two days earlier, I would have filled the blank between those words with *hates*.

Like mine, a pair of beds occupied the cell directly

across from me. I looked down the hall in both directions but could not see much with the bars there. All was quiet.

"Hello?" I asked.

"Archer?" the voice called again. "That you?"

"Yeah," I answered. "Who's this?"

"It's Draven. I saw them bring you in, man. Your head was bleeding pretty bad. You alright?"

Draven was an old friend of mine.

Yeah." I shook my head in confusion. "I think so. Were you calling my name earlier?"

"Sure was, but you were out cold. Anthony's with me. Anthony Taylor."

Anthony was a fighter from Britain. I used to call him Chocolate Thunder jokingly. He did not like it at first, but I think it grew on him.

They were both professional fighters. Some of the best I had seen besides myself in years, and we had been friends since the moment I met them. I did not like too many people, but I wanted Draven and Anthony as friends, saying a lot about them, good or bad.

"Draven?" I asked. "Anthony? What's… Who's…?"

A third voice in the near distance let me know there were others. A few other people were talking. I could not make out what they were saying and listened for a moment as my eyes came around.

"Hey..." another voice chimed in. "Who's there?"

We ignored it. They were not part of the conversation, not yet.

"Where are we?" I asked.

"I ain't got even the slightest clue, man," answered Draven. "I can't remember anything. And I mean jack-shit. Nada. Like fucking nothing."

I paced back and forth across the cell a few times and stopped to grab the bars again. My grip tightened. I pulled to test their hold and found them to be as strong as they appeared.

"Anthony," I called.

"What up, Big Man?" answered Anthony.

"You remember anything?"

"Yeah."

"How'd you get here?"

"Noticed these two guys following me around the other day and—"

"The other day?" I interrupted. "How long have you been here?"

"'Bout five days," answered Anthony, "I think. Five days without food's got me ready to kill a bitch up in here. Ya' feel me?"

My gut wrenched just thinking about it. "Five days? You mean they don't feed you? They don't bring you anything?"

"Not a damn bite in the three days I've been here," said Draven.

"That's right," said Anthony, "and dat' Jean Bean dude a couple of—"

"Jean Bean?" I interrupted again.

"White boy, four or five cells over. Fighter from

another country. He was already here when I got here. I know that cat's starvin."

All three of us were former fighters, four including Jean. And we all knew each other. Nothing about it made sense.

"Anyhow," continued Anthony, "I dipped around the corner of the next building while they were following me and eased into a little inset where they could not see my ass. Knew they were up to something shady because I'd seen them the day before. When they walked past me. Bam. I stole the motha'fuckas. Two days later, I was at home. Grabbed a bottle of water from the fridge, and the next thing I knew, I was tipsy. Figured I'd drank too much out at The Blue Room in Burbank and laid down. Woke up here, Big Man. That's it."

"Who are these people?" I asked.

"Don't know. How 'bout you? How'd they get ya'?"

"Someone hit me in the back of the head," I answered. "Felt like a pistol."

An alarm wailed out when I pulled my hands from the bars. I thought I had somehow set it off and glanced around for clues as flashing red lights oscillated in my fancy new cage. I wanted to rip the damn things from the ceiling and shove that speaker the alarm was blasting from up someone's ass. Anyones'. It was killing my head.

CLANK-CLANK.

I winced as the clanking sound echoed and the bars unlocked to open cells around us. My hand went subconsciously to my temple, seeking shelter from the pain. Each cell's occupants peeked cautiously out as the bars slid to the side for them to exit. I did not seem to be the only one disoriented. The rest or those behind bars exited slowly.

7-2
THE OTHERS

I stepped into the walkway beyond our opening bar doors. Kat Kelly's beautiful ass came into view. Another fighter. Pretty girl. Tall and lean with a Thai-boxer's build; she was a tough little bitch but sweet to no end.

She had long since been a friend of me, Elias, and Christy. Why she started dating him after he got caught fucking my wife and ruined my marriage is beyond me. I had not spoken to either of them since, though I held nothing against Kat.

"Kat?" I asked, surprised to see her.

Several soldiers in unfamiliar black, white, and grey digital patterned uniforms lined the hall to my right. They were heavily armed. One stepped forward while the others stepped in behind him.

"Start walking and stay quiet," he said.

She turned to see me. "Archer? What's going—"

"No talking," said one of the soldiers.

She looked at me for a moment with shaking eyes. We both had questions we would not have answers to for a few days. All we could do was listen to the soldiers directing us and walk.

Keith Reynolds, David Brat, and Roger Pendleton exited from a few cells down the way and took timid strides into the walkway. Roger's hands were shaking. None of us knew what the fuck was going on or why we were surrounded by bars walking a concrete floor under low set ceilings.

A pattern was developing: We were all current or former MMA fighters, wearing orange prison clothes, and none of us knew what the hell was going on. I was alone in having experienced being a captive. The others... They were tough, but they had never been soldiers or sampled the spices death and war have to offer, much less been held captive as I have.

"David," whispered Keith, "how'd we get here?"

"No clue, brother," answered David. "Not a goddamn clue."

We gathered to share the same unspoken thoughts. Everyone was quiet. There was no point in talking. Each of our eyes told the same story, and it was nothing that could change the situation.

Romulo Garcia, a heavyweight, Brixton Coxx, some French fucker, and Reece Ochoa—an American Indian fighter that used to claim he fought to represent 1st nation—exited their cells to move in behind us.

"This is fucking bullshit," shouted Reece.

A soldier smashed him in the back of his knee with the butt of his rifle, and he buckled. "I said no talking."

I almost laughed. Watching Reece grunting from the ground as he picked himself up felt like a gift. He was not my favorite person there, and he deserved it—payback for being a prick.

Reece was the only one there unworthy of respect. Liars are not my thing, and he was about as big as they came. He claimed native heritage, Comanche, to gain popularity as one of the few full-blooded Indian fighters, even got the tattoos to back it. Of course, once it came out that he was a full-blooded Mexican, he denied it and turned his back on his parents when they came forth with proof. He was a piece of shit.

A clicking door interrupted my thoughts as I gave Reece the evil eye. Footsteps followed. A group of armed soldiers was making their way down the narrow hallway, and they were not coming to bake cookies with us.

A speaker high above our cells activated, and a female voice spoke, "Please continue to the recreation area."

The armed soldiers herded us without a word. We knew what to do, devoid of needing them to say it. Again, a gunshot sounds the same in every language.

I caught the name tag on the man leading them as he approached. He was a Lieutenant:

"BRICE"

Lieutenant Brice and the other soldiers ushered us towards a large open area coming into view beyond a pair of double doors held open by two soldiers.

"Stop so these soldiers can take an image of your pretty faces before you pass through," said Lieutenant Brice.

One by one, we reached them and had our faces read

by handheld biometric scanners before passing through the doors.

"What's this really for?" I asked as a soldier scanned me.

"Facial recognition." Lieutenant Brice pointed to an overhead camera. "Now, keep walking."

I eyed the camera before cutting Lieutenant Brice a look to let him know what I thought about him before entering.

7-3
THE OPEN AREA

We were in some sort of rec room. Extensive walls and high crème-colored ceilings with patches of yellow and burnt orange outlined the scene. A dozen tall chairs stood around a 20-foot stainless-steel table. For reasons beyond my comprehension, its trimming was brown henna inlaid with gold and an expensive piece of furniture in stark contrast to the cellblocks they were holding us in.

The soldiers forced us to one side of the room, the empty side.

"Shit," said Reece.

"Keep your mouths shut," said Lieutenant Brice.

"Make me?"

Lieutenant Brice pointed his rifle at Reece. "I have a better idea."

He had a look in his eyes familiar to me. Any doubts in my mind he would not pull the trigger fled me.

"Okay," said Reece. "Fine. It is cool."

Dumbass. I would have been fine with Lieutenant Brice shooting the fucker.

A man with a three-star general's uniform and a stern face saying he was not particularly good with jokes entered the scene. I recognized him from my first call to duty as Captain Warwick, only now he is just another asshole entering to control us like beat animals. Five heavily armed soldiers entered the open area with him.

The man that followed had me wanting to knock someone out, as Romulo, Brixton, and Reece whispered amongst themselves. I was shocked to see him, which doesn't happen often, and in disbelief. He stopped at the center of the room with Captain Warwick at his side.

"Good evening," he said. "I'm—"

"Captain Shepherd," I interrupted.

He pointed to the stars on his uniform. "Close, but it's General Shepherd now. Hello, Archer. And, like always, I'm in charge here. I'm sure you already figured that out."

"In charge of what exactly, sir? What's this all about?"

"Such a loyal soldier. I always liked that about you, Master Sergeant Kemp. But that's only half of why you're here. You're missing the real question."

"Hey, man," said Draven, "I want my phone call. I know my rights."

General Shepherd turned to Captain Warwick

and raised his brows. "Captain Warwick, you did read Draven his rights, correct?"

"Negative." Captain Warwick shook his head. "Not so much anyway."

"The only rights you have here, young man," said General Shepherd, "are the ones I give you. At the present moment, that equals exactly zero."

Kat stepped forward.

"Why us?" she asked.

"Why a bunch of fighters?" answered General Shepherd. "And not just any fighters, but the very best? Well, this opportunity is unique, and at the risk of sounding cliché, I'm going to give you a chance to be all that you can be."

"Listen," said Kat, "you can't just—"

Lieutenant Brice crossed my path and pushed Kat back into the group. She fell hard.

I latched onto the outside of his left wrist and twisted it up behind him with one hand while removing the pistol from his holster with the other. The back of his knee buckled forward when I jammed the bottom of my foot into it. Lieutenant Brice did not like it, but he said nothing with the barrel of his gun against his eyelid.

Kat stood and kicked him in the side of the head. "Keep your hands off me."

As I said, she is one tough little bitch.

The other soldiers raised their weapons. Everyone in tacky orange was a target, but so was Lieutenant Brice after I rested the barrel where his hairline used to be.

General Shepherd forced a grin. "Hold your fire."

He eased to the other side of the room with calm strides considering I had a pistol against Lieutenant Brice's forehead. He still had control of the situation. He understood there was nothing to worry about on his end. I could not pull the trigger without everyone else getting shot.

"I'm not so sure you that you've thought this out quite yet, Kemp," he continued. "I taught you better than this. Think about what you're doing and the situation you're in. Unless you want to be responsible for the death of these people, and I mean all of them, I suggest that you drop that weapon."

I removed the magazine, set the pistol down, kicked it to his feet, and tossed the magazine across the floor next to him. It was the smart thing to do.

Lieutenant Brice gathered himself from the floor, smirking before he picked up his rifle and cracked Kat in the face with it. It knocked her out cold. I was the only one that did not flinch, but not everyone in the room had war in their hearts.

A butch-sexy flyweight fighter made famous by TMZ for scrapping with others in public stepped up to the plate with a tone that matched her mindset. "Listen, you son of a mother—"

"Haley Davenport," interrupted General Shepherd, "where exactly do you think you are?"

She eyed him. I think she was trying to come up with something witty and be the voice of reason, but what was there to say? She knew no more than the rest of us.

General Shepherd motioned to his soldiers. "Take her away."

Kat was waking, bleeding, and dizzy when three soldiers restrained her with zip ties around her wrists and on both her ankles. She was too woozy from the blow to fight back. It was best that way. I wanted to do something but had to be patient.

"Welcome to The Tower, ladies, and gentlemen," said General Shepherd before turning to his men. "Captain Warwick…see the others to their quarters. If so much as one of them tries something like that again, shoot a few of their friends to give them something to think about."

General Shepherd walked out. It was a few minutes later before we were herded back to our cells at gunpoint—cattle for the slaughter pens left to dwell upon our fates until morning came.

I walked back to my hold that night with guns at my back and a bit of concern. It was not fear. It was worry. Some of the other fighters were scared, but that was understandable. They were not used to having death's barrel on them like I was. They were fighters. We all were, but only I was a war machine.

No one talked once we were back in our cells and the soldiers left. Sitting quietly in their own doubts hurt the other's morale and added to the gloom, but I recognized despair's origin. I could feel its aura in the air like unspoken and unified thoughts speaking silently in synchronization: '*We're all going to die in The Tower.*'

I was still fuzzy-headed and ready to sleep when I laid down, which was not long after my head hit the cot. Undoubtedly, the others were having a more challenging time falling asleep than I was, because my ass was out the instant I closed my eyes.

CHAPTER 8

MATRIMONY

I WANTED TO SNEAK back and see Christy the day we got married at her mother's church in San Diego, but she had already told me she would kill me if I saw her in the wedding dress before she walked the aisle. It happened to be a tradition I was glad to have in place. I did not need to see it. The thought of marrying was already rattling my nerves a little, but I was ready.

Marriage was nothing I had thought about before. I figured it was not for me until I met her. She accepted my tours of duty, the fact that I was often gone for months on end, that my job was dangerous and could leave her widowed someday, and—for reasons I will never understand—loved my sense of humor. She was perfect.

I was shaking with anticipation in the holding room event coordinators had me in, awaiting the wedding to start. To make things worse, nothing in eyesight looked to be worthy of distracting me from my nerves: an old-fashioned chair, blue carpeting, a bookshelf filled with everything but books, and a luxury vanity desk probably worth thousands, but I could not tell you the maker. I was alone with my thoughts.

"Big bro…" Elias opened the door and entered the room. "Ready for this?"

"Yeah," I answered. "I am. Never been so sure of anything in my life."

"Good." He shook my hand for a man-hug. "Glad to hear. She's great, man. At least one of us found something special on the beach that day, right?"

"You'll find someone, Elias. You're a high-profile fighter, got a little cash, and you're almost as handsome as I am. So—"

Elias punched me in the arm. "What?"

I took a fighting stance, and we moved around for a bit in a technical sparring match. We were laughing and tapping each other with caring blows until he shot in for a body lock, and we grappled for a moment. That tussle turned into an embrace.

"I love you, bro," said Elias.

"Back at you." I patted his back. "Love you too, but don't you go getting all mushy on me now."

His eyes showed signs of watering when he pushed me back to grab my shoulders and look me in the eyes. "You deserve this more than anyone I've ever met in my life. You really deserve this."

"Thanks." I smiled. "Whatever happened to her friend anyway?"

"Julie? Girl's crazy."

"I know. I know. She's going to be here today."

His eyes widened. "For real?"

"Nah. I'm just kidding."

"Jesus, Archer. Don't do that."

I was cracking up before he finished his sentence, laughing harder than I had in a while.

Elias and Julie dated for a bit after we met them on the beach that day. A month later, they had already separated because Elias could not take her jealousy any longer, but it did not stop her. She even invited him over one day, claiming she wanted to '*formally apologize and let it go*,' only to stab his car tires to keep him from leaving.

He saw her doing it from the window and went out the back door, fearing he would be next. Wise call. After that, she went to jail only to stab another inmate with a fork and get time added to her sentence. Julie, however, somehow got out early for good behavior.

She was released a few weeks before our wedding. It made it funnier to tease him about it. As it turns out, Christy had only known her a week before we met them on the beach that day.

Elias's alarm went off on his phone. He looked at it and paused.

"What?" I asked.

"They're ready for you, Archer." He hugged me. "She's a lucky lady."

"Glad you think so."

"I know so." He grabbed my arm, turned me to fix my tie, and led me from the room. "Come on. Let's go get you hitched."

8-2
HONEYMOON

The reception had been friendly, but nights that followed in the Yosemite National Park were twice that. We had a room reserved on the top level at the Ahwahnee hotel two thousand feet from the base of Yosemite Valley. It was not something you would find in the high-end suites of Vegas. It was better.

The room was rustic with handmade, brown wooden chairs across the room from a king-sized bed. Christy made sure to point it all out to me, detailing the room down to its brownish tan leather headboards and rug over the darkened hardwood flooring.

"See," she smiled. "It even matches the bed."

I did not care too much about its décor, but Christy was happily talking about it. That's all I needed to know to care. I loved what she loved. Period.

"You plan on going into decorating," I smirked, thinking about the overly drawn-out details she was giving me, "Or are you maybe marketing this place for extra income in the future or something?"

"Why not?" Her posture changed as she straightened her clothes to get into character. "If you'll step over here, you'll see a sliding glass door." She placed her hand on it. "It's currently holding back the cold but gives way to a beautiful balcony made of large pieces of timber measuring over a foot thick. The view beyond its log rails brings to life a Californian landscape in its sharpest state. From here you can see large pines with snow-tipped branches matching the Ahwahnee's snowy ground a few stories below as powdered mountain tops peek over tall trees mighty in stature; and, if you were to step outside, you'd be breathing air cleaned to perfection by nature under a faultless baby blue sky. There's also the fireplace you see here at the foot of the bed giving a—"

"Stop," I broke into laughter. "What's wrong with you, goofball?"

She nodded and smiled proudly. "You've got to admit it was pretty good."

"Okay." I nodded playfully. "I'll give you that."

"You better say it was good." She winked. "Why don't you run us a bath while I unpack?"

"Now that…" I paused. "That sounds like an excellent idea."

Christy lit the fireplace and started unpacking while I ran her a candlelit bubble bath in a tub intended for two, dropping in a pair of lavender bath balls under spout as it filled. They were her favorite. I smiled at the thought of her obsession with them as I watched the tub fill with warm water.

She entered behind me as I stopped its flow to wrap me in a loving embrace. Her breath on the back of my collar… The scent of her mouth… She was undressing me. Shirt. Shoes. Pants. Socks. Boxers. She turned me as if to taste from her knees, but I pulled Christy to her feet and became lost in green eyes while sampling flawlessly pouty lips.

The sliding glass door remained cracked for nature's ambiance in the other room, but we had a fire going to hold cold air at bay. I switched our positions and undressed Christy from behind. Her skin called for my teeth to bite gently into it, but I held back to bolster her desires. I wanted her…*to want.*

Water warmed our bodies when we entered the tub. I slid behind Christy to nestle her in, wrapping her left earlobe between my lips as her back warmed my chest. Our heartbeats fell into an indistinguishable rhythm.

I bathed my love, and her head rolled with movements coaxed by strong hands cradled unspoken desires as they cleansed. She cherished every brush of the cloth and, I think, wanted its barrier removed for skin-to-skin contact. Extasy assembled between us.

Desire built rapidly, but I refused to rush it. We placed passion above all else and never skipped little pleasures; because fleeting hands crush beautiful moments. Patience was key.

"I love you, Archer," said Christy.

I tugged her hair to the side and kissed a sharp jawline that cut into my soul. “And I love you as well.”

Her hips swayed a tender backside into me and shifted my blood flow with subtle movements. Her breaths shuttered. She was ready, and all but asking me to step from the tub—an unspoken wish fulfilled. I lifted Christy from its waters to carry her into a firelit room with an already warming bed.

The love of my life was lost and missing from reality when she molded herself into the mattress. Her eyes fluttered, willing me to find her, but I was already there. She was the only love I knew.

The taste of her flesh… I had never taken so much time finding her. Her arms, tips of her fingers, her legs, and across her toes, she became a willing victim to lawful acts of seduction. But her neck beckoned me.

Everything on her became a target to slow-moving kisses, nibbles, licks, and gentle suction without release while shifting locations. I could feel her pulse, but I did not have to. It was beating its way from her chest with breaths struggling to match it.

The moment was unparalleled, and I could no longer tell where I ended, and she began.

Never had I savored magnificence before sipping it from her over the hours that followed. Time passed unnoticed and unspoken. It was observing.

A few hours later, we made love that would shake the Ahwahnee hotel’s foundation with hidden vibrations emanating from a tribal place in Christy’s soul, one she had yet to feel, one I had never felt before. Aftershocks rocked it further. I had placed her on a cloud high above before we made love to ensure she was there with me.

After another hour of being lost together, she moaned her final release as I begged my lover to stop moving until I could no longer handle her, and she collapsed on top of me. Our hearts slowed, and breathing returned normal. It was our most significant personal moment together.

We fell asleep in each other's arms with pleasure's moisture trapped between us.

CHAPTER 9

THE APE-LIKE MAN

I WAS HALF ASLEEP when they woke me, pulled me from my cell, and walked me through a series of corridors with armed soldiers surrounding me. It brought back a favorite memory of mine: my first title fight. Elias was exiting with me, and my team was in line behind him with their hands on each other's shoulders to form a support train.

Music blared as beams of light shot sporadically through a foggy haze. The energy was electric and lit me afire. My fans could not see me until I stepped through it, then they could only get a glimpse of my silhouette for a few moments until I emerged from the fog and flashing backlights.

People were cheering. Elias's hands on the back of my shoulders, though I had experience being locked alone in the cage for a no-holds-barred fight, let me know I was not alone.

The crowd's enthusiasm grew. Announcers were undoubtedly talking about my arrival, and the air warmed a few degrees as I passed through the smoke and sparks. My awareness swelled with each step to render me undefeatable.

No one could trump me. MMA champions' mindsets are that of unarmed killers who let go of chokeholds at the last second to avoid taking a life. But the walk I made that morning was not to a title fight. No one had their hands on my shoulders, and I was not walking an entrance ramp.

A tall entryway came into view. One of the soldiers pulled a key-fob from his pocket to swipe an entry pad. I squinted under the sun, but it was a price my body had to pay for going a few days without seeing a significant source of light. Its piercing brightness, however, was far less irritating than the cuffs overtightened on my wrist. They were burrowing into me as our destination came into view beyond the door.

They called it the yard, and it was amply named: an outdoor section atop a tower that felt like a prison. The walls were high, some 60 plus feet with razor wire-lined edges as if someone had a chance of reaching its topside.

There were no entry points besides the one I was at, not that I could see. Four sniper towers stood tall and menacing at each corner with a man perched and ready to fire. Surveillance cameras were everywhere—like we were stuck in a sadistic reality TV show with Big Brother watching.

One of the soldiers uncuffed me. I wanted us to be alone to shove the damn things up his ass and clamp the cheek plates to his prostate. He seemed like the kind of guy that would have liked it.

"Maybe later," I mumbled.

"What's that?' asked the soldier.

"Nothing."

The soldiers snickered as he walked me to the center of the yard. "Damn right, nothing."

He backed away and left me standing alone in light-colored dirt that reminded me of desert warfare. I observed the yard, wondering what the hell was about to happen until the sound of a door opening and shutting caught my attention. I turned to find General Shepherd emerging from one of the sniper tower's bases at the furthest side of the yard. Two soldiers covered him as he approached me. I would say he was lucky for it, but he was brilliant.

"Beautiful day," said General Shepherd. "You know, Master Sergeant, you were always my pick. My favorite. They advised against it. Damaged goods, they said, but they don't know you like I do. Not as a soldier. I'll even go so far as to say I followed your fighting career. You were an unstoppable force, Archer, even in the octagon. I think we can both agree that I get credit for a lot of that. After all, I made you. You're welcome for that."

"You've always been an arrogant prick," I said. "My

mother made me. I don't know what you're up to, but I've got a kid back home who needs me."

I rubbed my wrists. The cuffs had left their mark on both skin and nerve endings.

"I'm sure you have questions," said General Shepherd. "Feel free to ask."

"Okay then." I adjusted my feet, raised my hands, and shifted my body to a ready position before tucking my chin. "Why don't you take a few more steps forward? Let's settle this shit once and for all. You know, call it a day?"

"Maybe another time." He smiled. "I'd say your plate's pretty full at the moment."

"You abduct what," I asked, "twelve, thirteen of the most high-profile mother fuckers in the world, the most famous fighters walking the planet whose faces are plastered all over the T.V. and internet, and you think no one's going to notice or come looking for them?"

"Looking?" He laughed. "Oh, they're looking. It's an all-out manhunt, in fact. Will they find you? I don't think so. Not here. And by the time I'm done with you, you honestly won't care. Who knows? You may even thank me for it."

That is when things started to get weird. And by weird, I mean fucked up. A large and screwed-up-looking man, which still resembled a human, came from the same door I had. A dozen armed soldiers were guiding it with Captain Warwick in tow.

The once-man thing strolled towards me and

stopped 20-feet away to become motionless. He had patches of missing hair on his head and eyes like an unwell animal. They had done something to him.

I scanned the yard again. Soldiers were on standby, focusing on me as that messed-up man walked my way again. His skin was dry and ready to crack. The gait was off in his steps. I took two slow steps back and stopped when he ceased his advance, hunched in wait, and stared as if he were empty inside. His brow was thick and hairless. It protruded from his forehead and wrapped his eyes to reach high over equally bulging cheekbones. His nose was fat with offset ridges. Tendons in his neck stretched to his shoulders.

"Whoa." I took a step back. "You're one ugly son of a bitch. What the hell did they do to you?"

I knew what was about to happen. Shit was going to hit the fan. I clenched my fists tight, and my knuckles cracked under pressure hoping to be the fan.

That man… That thing in front of me shifted posture for an attack.

I glanced at General Shepherd. "So, it's going to be like this?"

"I'm afraid so." He took a few steps back. "Attack."

The large man charged me, touching his knuckles to the ground once and moving like man and ape. He was more than ruthless. He was rabid. I countered with an unpleasant right hard enough to hurt my knuckles and side-stepped with a leg kick as he passed by. My shinbone buried past flesh and into the femur beneath his thigh, but it did not hurt the son-of-a-bitch.

I will never forget the first time he hit me. I had never felt such power—he tried to shut down my brain for maintenance. I was in trouble.

He was massive and robust yet moved with grace and precision. Every time I thought I was about to shine or thought I was doing something right, that man, that thing cast shadows upon my efforts. He overwhelmed me with power alone, and I no longer felt like I was fighting a man.

I eventually delivered a blow that hurt him: a straight into the esophagus, like the one I hit the punk in the alley while looking for Christopher but with more force. It was my go-to when things got nasty. It even dropped him. I thought the fight was over until he pushed himself to his hands and knees from the dirt and looked at me with unbridled anger in his eyes.

"Well…" I turned to General Shepherd for a second. "I've managed to piss it off."

General Shepherd laughed. "That you have."

At least someone thought it was funny.

I took a step, and soccer kicked him in the face when he started to rise, but he kept rising with big angry breaths. The kick left his jaw warped to the side and locked into place. I hear a broken mandible hurts like hell. It must have been true. He was wincing.

Man or beast, he stood with deliberately slow movements to bask in the joy of what he was planning. He still wanted to fight. I had to respect it, though it was not something I found settling.

I rushed him before he could gather himself, only to be tossed across the yard like a rag in a dog's mouth and left sliding to a stop some 30-feet away. He was on me before I could get back to my feet, smashing like an ape with abnormal levels of anger.

He hammered me into the ground, and there was not a damn thing I could do about it. I tried, but every impact rippled through my body like someone was beating me with a sedan. They were blows not meant to be taken and survive.

I managed to sweep him off-balance at one point. It was not luck, but it was not something I had planned either. It was survival instinct at best.

He rolled to his stomach to push himself up, but I beat him to my feet to line him up for another kick to the face. It did not go as hoped. He grabbed me by the ankle as he stood and snatched my legs out from under me, spinning me around several times before releasing me like an Olympic hammer-toss competitor going for gold.

I landed some 40-feet away the second time he tossed me and slid across the dirt again. My head was heavy due to pressure from him spinning me before my release.

"The fuck is this thing?" I asked myself.

I tried to stand, but nothing was working right. My body was not listening anymore. Getting to my hands and knees felt impossible, but I could not stop. I knew that thing would kill me if I did.

I got my right foot under me. Everything appeared filtered through a blurry red haze. I could no longer tell if I was facing him. My eyes were blood-sodden.

I could hear him pounding his chest and smashing the ground. He was coming at me again, and I was half-dead. Dust must have flown when his knuckles hit the dirt on the charge—because the ground shook.

An impact on my upper back sent my chest slamming into the Earth. Flashes of light blinded me further with every shot. They were so hard that I could not even feel them anymore. I could only hear the impacts. That is how one knows they are in real trouble when they can no longer feel the damage their body is taking.

I was nearly motionless, but he would not stop—savagery at its finest. He was beating me to death, and I was powerless.

The world around me slipped away until I could barely hear the beating it was throwing me. Then, a few seconds later, I could no longer hear. Ape-like smashes and aggression were finally handing me peace. I could feel my brain shutting down. 95% of me was worried about my son. The other five percent was glad to die, but thoughts of Christopher let me know I did not want to die as bad as I thought I did. It is something I should have realized sooner, but it was too late to take it back.

General Shepherd shouted something as it beat me. I was unable to hear, but he yelled it again. A few seconds later, a faint gunshot rang out, and I was gone.

CHAPTER 10

FAMILY MAN

A GREY OVERCASTING SKY provided the perfect picnic in cooling gusts of Georgia air. Christy and I had our son, Christopher, by then. He was seven years old and tearing into almond butter and raspberry jelly sandwiches with sliced bananas while talking with his mouth full.

"This kid at my school," said Christopher, "he's so skinny, and all he eats is salads and fruits and stuff because his mom and dad are vegan, I think. I always tell him to eat these because they fill you up, but he doesn't like peanut butter, and he doesn't listen. So, I told him he would never get bigger and that one day I'll let him wear my old clothes from now if we were still friends when we grow up to be adults."

Christy and I giggled. He was always saying things off the wall.

"Where do you come up with stuff like that?" asked Christy.

"Gets it from you," I answered.

"Yeah," she laughed. "We all know that isn't true."

"Yeah, mom," said Christopher. "I get it from you. Duh."

A lizard scampered by the old oak tree at our side, and he got up to move for it. He obsessed over them.

"He ever catch one of those things?" I asked.

"Once or twice." Christy watched him. "If you'd stop touring, you'd be here to find out."

"Come on." I pulled her into me and held her. "That's not fair. Besides, I'm done in four more years."

"Shouldn't have enlisted for another round."

"But I did. And you know why."

"Yeah. The perks are nice, but I'd rather have you home."

"I'm done after this one," I said. "I promise."

She squared up with me on the picnic blanket. "But do you mean it?"

"All the way. Maybe I'll become a farmer after."

"Yeah, right." She giggled and pinched my stomach.

I buried myself into her and tickled her hips, causing her to laugh harder.

"You couldn't grow a cactus." She laughed.

I tackled her to the checkered blanket next to a bottle of red wine and a woven basket—one she just had to buy for the picnic experience. "Saying I'm not good with my hands?"

"Oh honey," she said, "I'd never say that. Trust me."

I smiled.

"But you can't grow anything for crap," she continued. "Remember the—"

"Yeah, yeah," I interrupted, "but after I'm done with this stint, I'll have plenty of time to figure out my cactus garden. Wait and see."

"I bet you will." Christy gave my cheek a brush as she looked up at me, losing herself in my eyes and pulling me into her lost world. "Wanna get some practice with those hands later?"

I was too busy smiling to answer, but she earned a kiss after I looked to make sure Christopher was still preoccupied with the reptilian wildlife. A cool breeze slipped between our lips each time they parted but could not chill the fire between us. We had always been passionate. Every day was like the first.

"Gross," said Christopher. "Get a room already."

We were laughing before our lips parted to look his way, but Christopher was already back to chasing his lizard of choice.

"Isn't he just a little party pooper?" asked Christy.

"He's good at it, huh?" I asked in return.

"Too good." She smiled.

"Come on." I stood. "You ready to get out of here?"

"Nah." She looked Christopher's way and pulled me

back down. "Let's let him tire himself out a little more so he'll fall asleep early, and we don't have to be so quiet."

"Good idea." I turned to Christopher. "Hey, brat. Bet I can jog around this park more times than you can."

"In your dreams," he said.

"Let's do it then. A trip to the ice cream parlor says I win."

"Oh…" he laughed. "It's on."

I stood and took off with Christopher at my side.

We jogged for nearly an hour before he started to sweat. His face was flushing red. The kid had heart. I could have kept going but pretended to be depleted of energy down to the last step I thought he could make and collapsed seconds before he did.

"I…" He struggled on his back for air. "I won."

I watched the clouds passing overhead. The sound of his breathing and Christy cheering for him brought a smile to my face. Those were the moments I lived for. I loved being a family man more than I did a soldier.

CHAPTER 11

LAB RAT

I HAVE HEARD PEOPLE talk of NDEs in war, those out-of-body moments before death. I never believed in it, not until the day they strapped my lifeless body to that table and pumped me full of fuck-all.

It was far from a clear image, more like staring through heat waves into a mirage during a desert war; only I was strapped to a lab table. Both my legs were restrained at the ankles, knees, and thighs. A taut strap around my hips matched the one crossing my chest. I could not move, not that I had the strength to—if I were in control of my body at that point.

IVs were plugged into each of my arms. I was dying, yet somehow floating above my own body. The high-tech hybrid operating room they had me in came into view. They were about to do something to me, but I did not know what.

I watched as a medical assistant finished the final touches in securing my forehead with a thick strap to hold a mouthpiece deep into my throat. A breathing machine guided my chest to rise and fall. I think I was in a coma.

Some Chinese bitch I would soon know as Dr. Suyin entered in a white lab coat. She looked at the other two in the room. I knew them through many years working with the government: one American, Dr. Alin, and a Russian, Dr. Strogolev.

Dr. Suyin prepared a bright red serum at a stainless-steel station, waving it with little circles to mix and examine its contents.

"Dr. Strogolev," said Dr. Suyin, "I was thinking about the conversation that we had earlier. As I was saying to you and Dr. Allen, the debate on genetically modifying humans is old, but the milestones that we're crossing here are going to build the foundation for greater things."

"I understand that," said Dr. Strogolev, "but we've crossed a few lines here. If I'm being honest, the possibilities still frighten me."

"It's been a risky road for Dr. Kepler," she replied. "There's no room for us to doubt about it. No second-guessing. We must continue to expect resistance as his research progresses. I believe in what he's doing, and he's right when he says the benefits outweigh the risks."

Dr. Strogolev walked to the other side of the lab with a deep breath. He was not a man at ease with what he was doing. Dr. Suyin watched as he paced.

"Inserting genes from the human brain into an animal's is one thing," said Dr. Strogolev. "Inserting an animal's genes into a human is… Well, it's something different now, isn't it?"

"Dr. Strogolev—"

"I know what you're going to say, interrupted Dr. Strogolev, "but we're not intended to survive that way. These things are unpredictable, like wild animals. You can have a wolf for a pet too, but if you wake up the next day and your child is missing, you can't place the blame on someone else. I don't ever want that feeling."

"LS8 will see to it that our kids are safe," interjected Dr. Alin. "This I promise you. It'll improve the way we survive as a species. Attaching the new DNA variants with Kepler's LS virus is a crucial link in the emergence of human intelligence in animals as well as animal attributes to humans. There'll be risks, sure. It's inevitable. But if someone's going to win a Nobel Prize for something like this, I'd like that someone to be us. Otherwise, I'd feel—" His head whipped to the door. "Dr. Kepler…"

The others grew quiet when he entered. They tried to hide it but were jittery on edge in Dr. Kepler's presence. They stopped talking. Their bodies became tense.

The shadows of the laboratory concealed his face, but he moved into the light enough for me to catch a glimpse of his skin. Patches of gray and pale white peppered it. No hair was on his head. It was not shaved; it was just missing. The back of his neck on either side of his head had strange, bloated pockets like air-filled tumors that swelled—breathing independently over a multitude of dark black veins. They spider-webbed up and around his neck to fully encompass his head.

The skin on his hands looked like it was about to crack when he moved a mouse to click an icon on the monitor. The computer screen cleared itself of all but a password box, and he entered a long password that prompted him to voice recognition.

"Emil Kepler," he said.

Another prompt came up, and a biorecognition panel folded into view at the right of his keypad. He placed his palm on the scanner and a program file opened on the desktop.

A synthesized voice filled the room.

"Welcome, Dr. Kepler."

He continued working at the computer as he spoke to the others. "I do not ignore your concerns or fears, but you are familiar with the term speciation?"

"You're referring to Darwin's theory of evolution," answered Dr. Strogolev. "Favorable adaptations accumulate in a species, and bad ones disappear. The accumulated changes become so great that the result is an entirely new species."

"Precisely," said Dr. Kepler.

"But this is said to happen over generations."

"Biological evolution is a consequence of four factors," explained Dr. Kepler. "Overproduction, competition, genetic variation, and natural selection. LS7 has produced spectacular results bridging that generational pace in just seven stages. We're so close. Have no doubts. We have already created a pathway for humankind to become something better. Something connected, and not just to each another, but to the earth itself. They just don't know it yet."

"Someone better be telling that to the suits," said Dr. Strogolev. "I don't think patience or celestial utopias are at the top of their list."

Dr. Kepler never took his eyes or fingers off the computer and keyboard. I wanted to know what the red serum in the syringes next to my body was. Nor did I know about the DNA strands and other gibberish on the screen in front of him. The lab, everything, and everyone in it began to fade once they injected the red serum into the I.V. in my arm.

Their voices grew dim.

"I will deal with the suits," said Dr. Kepler.

Dr. Alan wiped my body down with iodine in preparation for whatever the hell was to come and turned to Dr. Kepler when he finished. "Doctor, we're ready for you."

Dr. Kepler completed his entries, pushed a button on a keyboard to bring up an exit prompt, and placed his palm on the sensor. The synthesized voice filled the room again.

"Logging out."

He opened a refrigeration unit. My eyes waned. A wall of vials containing varying shades of red liquid came into blurry sight as I watched from above:

'LS-1, LS-2, LS-3, LS-4, LS-5, LS-6, LS-7, LS-8.'

Dr. Han Suyin pulled a few LS-8 VIALS out and placed them on the counter next to her. Dr. Kepler grabbed one. Reality was getting hard to distinguish from my approaching dream state. I did not know if it was real or not, but his fingers were strange: wiry, dangling, grayish-white, and vascular.

He gently placed the vials into a stainless-steel briefcase.

General Shepherd filled the doorway. "How'd it go?"

"Any worse shape, and you would be burying him," answered Dr. Kepler. "I thought he was your prize."

"I knew you could fix him."

Dr. Kepler continued packing up the LS vials. "Thanks to LS8, yes."

"What are you doing with those vials?"

"Organizing."

Their words were getting harder to make out on my slow descent into the end of everything.

General Shepherd eyed him for a moment. "I'm getting threats from the Pentagon. They're losing patience."

"One cannot rush perfection," said Dr. Kepler.

"Proceed. Start wi** *** ***** **** *****."

I could no longer make out the words, but I recall the blurry image of his eyes as the NDE ended, and I drifted back towards myself: they were dark and off-colored. I wanted to check them out a bit longer, but that is all I remember.

CHAPTER 12

LETTERS FROM HOME

RECEIVING MAIL FROM loved ones at Camp Victory in Bagdad is not a speedy process. Christy had not written as much as she had in the past, but I expected it from time to time. Life happens.

I was laying on my bunk doing jack-all when Kyle, a squadmate of mine over the last two tours, brought in the mail and passed it out to everybody. He tossed the envelopes like Chinese throwing stars. I dare say he was unusually good at it.

"Ninja in a past life?" I asked.

"Nah," answered Kyle, "but I was into that stuff when I was a kid making paper throwing stars. Started buying real ones to throw into the sides of trees. Kid stuff. I just never stopped throwing them."

"You never grew up," I laughed. "Why do you keep them in your bag?"

"Okay. You got me." He walked off. "I'm a closet ninja through and through."

I shook my head and scanned my letters. There were two from the state I did not bother opening. I knew what they were. They were confirmation letters for government checks received that had built up six months—payment for shedding blood.

A letter halfway through the pile caught my attention. Familiar handwriting. It was from Christopher.

"Be nice to get at least one from Christy," I mumbled to myself.

I opened the letter from Christopher with the blade of my knife while admiring his young yet quickly developing handwriting:

> *"Hi daddy its Christopher and I miss you. We are having lots of fun here at home and I love you and I wish you were here so much. When are you coming back? I got good grades on my work at school and you would be proud of me. Mom doesn't know I sent this because I want to tell you something. I saw mommy and Elias in the bedroom naked together and I know you are coming home soon and this makes you mad and sad but don't be mad at me. I just want to tell you. I hope you are not too mad and I'm very very very sorry but*

wanted you to know. I love you and see you soon.

Love you daddy.

Christopher."

I went numb inside. I did not move or respond to anyone for the rest of the evening. It was the first time I kicked back beers since I was eighteen, and I sent more down my gullet than should have. It is not something I thought about doing. I reached for a squad mate's twelve-pack of piss water and started drinking.

If it were true and Christopher was not mistaken, I figured my brother was already practicing how to spit out his teeth for my return. The situation would be bad enough if she cheated on me, more so if she did it with my brother. And even more so if my son walked in and caught it in his eyes.

12-2
STUMBLING

I was shit-faced before the night was up. I drank more that evening than I had in ten years. It made things worse. I was having a hard time walking, and my voice slurred when I tried to speak.

I never stopped drinking after that. My son's letter was a catalyst to alcohol endeavors and hate. It threw my only fear into my lap. I was not weak-minded, but my heart had always been soft in Christy's hands. She and Christopher were my world, and thoughts of losing them, to my brother of all people, was too much to bear.

The night progressed until anger took over rational thoughts. It was the first time I had ever thought about hurting myself. I did not do it, of course, but the idea was there.

Someone I could not remember to save my life tried to take a bottle of whatever the fuck I was on at that point from me, and I tried to hit him, only to miss and fell flat on my face. Neither balance nor depth perception were in my corner.

Kyle pulled me off to the side of the building around 3:00 AM to save me from starting a scene with a few squadmates of mine. I do not remember what I got so riled up about, but I am sure it was something stupid. They were most likely trying to help me with what I was going through.

I puked at Kyles feet halfway through our chat. "I'm…I'm sorry.

"I'll be right back," said Kyle. "I'm going to go get you some water. Stay here. Don't move."

12-3
DIRTY SHEETS

He left, and I must not have listened. The next thing I knew, I was waking up in bed with a nauseous feeling. I moved to get up with lingering drunkenness to see my sheets covered in mud to match my bare feet. I had gone somewhere and not taken my shoes.

"That's interesting," I mumbled.

I made my way to the bathroom and spent a good five minutes on the toilet with a bad case of diarrhea. Thankfully, there was a nearby garbage can to puke in while I sat on my porcelain throne. It smelled… Well, it was not pleasant.

It took several glasses of water and a few salty breakfast burritos to get me feeling half right.

I drank until I was tipsy the next seven days remaining on my final tour but made sure not to get that wasted again. A lecture from my superior made sure of that.

There was going to be a lot of explaining when I got home the following week. The flight could not come soon enough, though I dreaded the possibility of learning the truth. My last week in the service was not pleasant, and I could only hope Christopher was wrong or wrote the letter to get attention from me, which I did not believe to be the case.

CHAPTER 13

STAPLES

I DO NOT REMEMBER waking up in the lab when Dr. Kepler and the other geeks finished with me, but I recall the walk back to my cell. It was hard. I felt heavy, and my veins pulsated with discomfort. Felt like jagged thorns charred down to partial embers were flowing through them.

That big fucker I fought in the yard jacked me up. I was in rough shape, but the red serum took its toll in a grander fashion. Though, I was not yet aware to what degree.

My whole body burned, and my vision was off. An iron scent covered any other smells in the area—a tell-tale truth of blood in my sinuses most likely due to getting my face pounded in. It was my first ass-whooping. One that let me know how I had left others to feel in the past.

I was walking dazed and almost certainly had a concussion or worse. My legs refused to cooperate with the signals my brain sent them. Every step was a challenge not to fall flat on my face.

Two armed soldiers escorted and partially carried me. We must have been walking thirty or more yards before I realized what was happening. It was another first for me to wake up sleepwalking and still half in a dream. The bottoms of my feet burned under the weight of my body.

We passed another group of soldiers coming from the opposite end of the hallway. They were pushing an unconscious man on a gurney, and we came to meet with them in front of an empty cell. Then he came into my hazy eyesight. I could not believe it. The red serum circulating my body must have had dream states at play.

"Eh…" I struggled. "Elias?"

"Yeah," said one of the soldiers. "Your brother. You guys are going to be neighbors."

"Elias," shouted Kat. "Elias…"

"Shut it," said one of the soldiers.

"Elias," she continued.

"I said shut it," he shouted.

His orders followed with the sound of a weapon chambering to fire. She quickly quieted when it happened, and I was glad she did. I was in no state to help her.

My eyes were glued to Elias as they opened my cell and the one beside it. I tried to say something more but could not get my mouth to move. They wheeled him into the other cell and helped me into mine.

The soldier at my back shoved me with his rifle's barrel. I landed on the cot. Well, I kind of landed on it. My knees hit the concrete. Pain streamed through my body like a blistering inferno until I was holding in screams.

A loud flopping sound of Elias hitting the cot in the cell next to me signaled they were no less gently transferring him. Bar ends clattered into a concrete edge and locked before the soldiers departed. I waited, listening to their footsteps until they dissipated to a faint pattern of nothingness.

An annoying scratching sensation dug at the back of my throat. It was a spiky dryness preventing me from calling out to Elias. My lips were stuck together and would not part. I strained to move them.

"Elias…" I barely whispered.

He did not reply, but Kat was trying to get his attention as well. Her face was pleading. I am sure she was scared for him. For herself. For all of us.

I struggled to raise my voice. "Elias…"

They must have drugged him like they had Anthony. It was no matter. He would not have been able to hear me anyhow. I could barely speak or hear myself when I called for him.

I looked to the bars and pulled myself the rest of the way onto the cot. Someone was going to die for the searing pain buckling me from the center of my head.

General Shepherd was a good candidate and at the top of my personal hitlist.

My side hurt when I rolled to it and clutched the back of my head. "What is this?" Something was there that did not belong. It felt like a piece of a belt, or something, was glued to my head, but that made no sense. I eased my fingers further down to the back of my head, brushing over small metal ridges. They were staples. Painful to the touch.

The lights went out. Faint, random screams reverberated the walls around us. Cries from unknown sources faded to the sound of silence as dim lights activated to illuminate my cell with an occasional flicker.

I laid back and closed my eyes, thinking about my son. He was the reason I was alive, the only reason I had not sent one of Buffalo Bore's 124-grain +P+ penetrator rounds burning through my skull at 1300 feet per second. Christopher was my savior, though he could not protect me from the red serum's effect on my central nervous system.

I was weak, and a slowing heart rate thumping in my ears told me I was far from out of the woods. There was nothing I could do but lay there. It was as good a day to die as any.

CHAPTER 14

KAT'S STORY

I SNAPPED OUT OF it sometime later, soaked in sweat, and sat up. My legs were hanging over the side of the cot. A drunken feeling overwhelmed me, only it was not the good kind of drunk. It was different, like poisoning from an unknown sedative.

"Shit," I muttered.

"Yo, Archer," said Kat. "You, okay?"

"Wondering that myself," said Roger, who I was beginning to think could not speak.

She was gripping the bars in her cell across the hall. She had a cut on her cheek and a head full of dried blood. Haley was lying on a nearby cot. Their cell was a mirror image of mine.

"Hey," I said.

I stood, mentally adrift from the beating and whatever they did to me back in that lab. I was already healing a bit from the fight, but not enough to think with a clear head. Not with that shit they put in me. Maybe it was healing me? Perhaps it was killing me? I had no way of knowing.

My breathing was labored as I moved to the cell's bars to talk with Kat.

"Where'd they take you?" I asked.

She shook her head. "You don't wanna know."

"Seriously," asked Draven, "what happened?"

Kat reflected for a moment. Anthony and Draven shifted position in cells across the way to listen as she paused, swallowed a lump, and turned her head towards the ceiling. She did not want to talk about it but knew we wanted to hear her story.

She was sharing a cell with Haley next to Draven and Anthony's on the left, directly across from me. To the right of them were Brixton Coxx and Reece, who I was not happy to have in eyesight. Everyone else was in cells I could only hear. Either way, I could see the curiosity on the faces of those in view. Anger swirled with sadness on Kat's.

"I don't know," answered Kat. "I don't know how I got there. I was hanging upside down from a hook with a rope around my ankles when a bucket of water splashing into my face woke me up. Then that Shepherd guy walked in talking about how things would not work around here without order. And how he respects me or some other bullshit like that. Guess I broke the order he was trying to keep socking that soldier."

Draven neared his cell's bars. "Shit, I'm glad you hit him."

"Not sure if it was worth it." Kat paused. "That's when the one they call Brice started shocking me with some damn taser thing until I passed out again. Next time I woke, I was back here in this cell. Did have a dream about Elias standing my ass up the night they snatched me, though."

"At least you know he had a good reason for it now," said Anthony. "You too dating again?"

"Hell no," she answered. "Just friends."

"How'd they get you?" I asked. "Where'd they take you from?"

"Bunch of guys jumped me when I was drunk and snatched me into a van. Got a few broken noses for their trouble, but I couldn't stop them. You?"

"They got lucky." I laughed, pausing to hold my head in pain. "Well, at least I know why you look like shit now."

She snickered. "You don't look so hot yourself, cowboy."

I exhaled in nearly empty thought. "You, okay?"

"Not really, unless you consider waking up in a frickin' prison and getting the shit kicked out of you by a couple of douchebags while hanging from a meat hook, okay. Then I'm peachy."

"Fuck that," said Brixton. "Fuck all this."

Kat angled for a better line of sight into the cell beside mine. "I still can't believe that's Elias next to you?

Well…" She paused. "Anthony's right. He did have a good excuse for leaving me hanging at the bar all night."

"Elias," I shouted, grabbing my head again.

The pain dropped me to a knee. Intense throbbing matched my pulse, telling me I needed to stay relaxed, but it was enough to wake my shitbag little brother.

"What the...?" Elias paused. "What's going on?"

"Elias…" Kat forced a smile. "Finally."

"Kat? That you? Where are we?"

"Yeah, it's me."

"Hey, Elias," called Anthony.

"Anthony?"

"Yeah. When I saw you, I was like damn, they'll let anyone up in this bitch."

"Jokes?" asked Draven. "Really?"

Draven and Anthony went back and forth for a bit, no doubt trying to get their minds off a messed-up situation. They even managed to get a few snickers from the others. My head hurt too bad to fund humor in it.

Not a word came from Elias as they talked. I could not blame him. He was most likely looking around his cell in confusion as to where he was. I did the same. Only I was not wondering why Anthony and Draven would be joking. Still, their conversation eventually died down to leave an awkward silence.

"Hey, little brother," I said after a moment passed.

"Archer? What's...? Are you guys playing some kind of joke on me?"

"Hello…" Draven waved at him from the cell on the

other side of the walkway. "We're right here with you, man. And no. This shit's far from a joke."

"Will somebody tell me what the hell is going on?" asked Elias.

"We're still trying to figure that out," answered Kat. "This asshole wants us to join the Army or something."

"No," I said. "That's not it."

Everyone stopped talking to listen. They knew I had been beaten half to death. Or to my end, I guess. It was apparent, but I had not talked about it.

"I saw the General kill a man today," I said. "Shot him in cold blood. At least I think it was a man."

"The fuck is that supposed to mean?" asked Draven.

"He was different. Huge. Never got a beating like that before."

Anthony stood and walked to the cell bars next to Draven with disbelief on his face and grabbed them. "You tryin' to tell me someone faded you like that in a one-on-one?"

The other prisoners moved to the edge of their cells, as far as the bars would let them for a better ear spot. I got why it was hard to accept. I was scrappy.

"Almost killed me," I continued. "I'm telling you, we're in trouble here."

"You look bad," said Kat, "but not beat to death bad."

"Strange, right? This morning I could barely move. I could barely breathe. They strapped me to a table. I think I had an NDE. I don't remember much after that, but now I feel damn good in comparison. They injected me with something. Some red shit."

A few of them moved to their cots in thought while others remained quiet near their entrapping bars. I sat with my back against my little brother's cell wall.

"Archer?" he asked.

"We haven't talked in five years, bro," I answered. "Why start now?"

After that, we did not say anything else, not until many hours had passed, and I could only assume night had fallen. There was no way to tell.

Draven and Anthony were lying quietly on their cots; Kat and Haley were doing the same. Soldiers patrolled the walkway for a while and moved to another area. I was still sitting with my back against that concrete wall when the lights went out.

I do not know why I spoke to him. But I did. "Hey…Elias."

"Hey," he answered. "Archer, I just want to say that I'm sorry about what I did."

"It's fine," I lied.

"I was just... It was a scumbag move. I should've—"

"That's not important right now," I interrupted. "We need to find a way out of here."

"No shit."

I moved to my bars. "I might have a plan if you want to hear it."

Elias moved to the edge of his cell. So did a few of the others. He could not see me beyond my hands extending from the cage, but it was enough to let him know he was not alone. I'm sure he, like the others, needed it.

"I'm down," whispered Elias. "Let's hear it."

"Me too," said Kat.

"I'm in," said Draven.

"Second me on that," said Anthony.

"Make that six of us," said Haley.

Reece, Roger, Brixton, Keith, Romulo, and Jean wanted in on the action as well, but I did not know them well or if they would turn coward when the time came. I told them I was okay with it, not that I had a choice whether they heard me talking with the others or not. I held no cares about it. That red serum was both taming me and giving me violent impulses at the same time. I felt calmer at heart than I had in years as I talked, but something primitive, something animal-like, was swelling within.

We talked all night—me, Elias, and the others—tweaking different game plans together we came up with and talking about their flaws, most of which were suicide disguised as hope. No one honestly believed we were getting out alive, but what's a man without his dreams?

"We need to get some sleep," I said. "Whatever hours we can before tomorrow. Never know what this place has in store for us."

"Agreed," said Kat. "I'm turning in."

Everyone was on the same page. We had developed

a plan to implement at some point that would, in all probability, get us killed, and we needed sleep. One by one, we laid ourselves down and tried to forget about what was happening. The cells grew quiet. I relaxed and let slumber take over.

CHAPTER 15

FLYING HOME

I DID NOT ENJOY the flight home after a week of thinking about Christopher's letter. Usually, I would have been excited. I am hard inside but not made of stone. I wanted to see my family, but I wanted to be happy when I did it.

A stewardess passed by with a cart full of drinks and snacks. "Can I get you anything?".

"Something to drink," I answered. "Vodka, maybe. Whiskey?"

"Here you go." She handed me a small shooter-sized bottle of vodka and a clear cup. "It'll be charged on the card you have on file for the flight."

"Thanks. Could I get a couple more?"

"How many?"

"Two?"

"Sure thing." She handed me two more bottles. "Enjoy."

She walked away, and I turned up a bottle, never bothering with the cup. It was nasty and felt like drinking rubbing alcohol. My lungs burned the first breath afterward.

I stared out the window in hopes of Christopher being wrong. Or that he was mistaken. But my gut told me otherwise. Christy had not written me in weeks. Before that, she would write a few times a week; and it did not matter whether I could get them and reply quickly.

My brother… It was hard to accept. Impossible. Elias would never do such a thing to me. He was the best man at my wedding and my best friend since childhood. There was nobody closer to me.

I must have stared out that window for an hour or more. Part of me felt like crying, but another part wanted to beat the shit out of somebody. The thought of what Christopher was, and was soon to go through if he were right, tore me apart. It was overpowering.

The stewardess passed by again. "Doing, okay?"

"Can I get another drink?" I asked.

"Same thing?"

"Let me try the bourbon this time."

"Sure."

"Three please?"

"Sorry. We have a five-per-flight policy. I can give you two."

"That'll work."

She handed me two more and let me be to drown myself.

15-2
FALLOUT

No one greeted me at the airport.

I exited the taxi under the Oregon Ash tree just outside our home on E. Tujunga Ave. in the hills of Burbank, California. The weather was nice, but it was the only thing pleasant.

I approached the front door to find Christy with most of her bags already packed.

"What the hell's going on?" I asked.

She didn't respond.

I called out to her again. "Christy?"

She came from the kitchen with a wide-eyed expression and froze in place. I watched her for a few seconds to study her nervous energy. My chest tightened with worry.

"Where's Christopher?" I asked.

"He's at my mom's house. Why?"

"For?" I asked.

She did not answer.

"Are you going to talk?" I asked.

"You're home early," she said.

"Yeah. I am. One day early." I motioned to the bags. "What's all this?"

She bit her nails. "I'm sorry, Archer." Her hand was shaking in her mouth. "I just can't do it anymore."

"Do what?" I took a shellshocked step back. "What the fuck are you talking about?"

"The tours, Archer." Her voice rose. "The tours. You're never going to quit, and I'm always going to be stuck here alone wondering if you're going to get killed and leave me to bury you and take care of a broken son."

I nearly walked out when I felt that wave of emotional panic hit me. "You knew what I did from the beginning."

"But you said you were going to stop. You never did."

"Listen." I paused to calm myself. "You can't just up and… I don't want you to—"

Elias entered the front door without knocking, stiffening when he saw me. "Archer…"

They looked at each other with nervous energy. That is when I knew Christopher was right. I had to ask.

"Are the two of you fucking?"

"No," answered Elias. "Come on, bro."

He was lying. I could always tell when he was. His posture would change, and he had this thing with his head where he looked away and back for a split second.

I turned to Christy. "You're a real bitch. You know that?"

"Archer," she said, "nothing happened between us.

Why are you acting crazy? Your brother's here to help me pack."

I turned to face him. "Then why didn't you write me and tell me what she was planning?"

"I just sprung it on him yesterday," interjected Christy.

"Bullshit!" I put my fist through the wall.

"Archer," said Elias, "you need to take a moment to—"

"Stop talking, Elias." I pointed my finger at Christy for a moment, too angry for words, then tossed the letter Christopher wrote me to the floor at her feet.

"What's this?" she asked.

A thousand-yard stare. That is all the bitch got from me. It was something she had never seen before.

She picked the letter up and read it. Tears followed.

"How do you feel now?" I asked.

"Christopher never said anything to me," she cried. "I never knew he saw anything or—"

"Or what?" I shouted. "Or that you were being a fucking whore."

"You don't have to call her a—"

I busted that piece of shit in his mouth halfway through his sentence. He fell through the front screen door, taking it down with him. Christy was screaming in the background as we fought over the railing and into the flower bed, trampling her roses. Elias was a formidable and well-trained fighter, but it ended with me stunning him with a hard right. The final blows left him helplessly punch drunk and wobbling against the side of the house.

"Why?" I hit him again. "How could you do this to me?"

Another shot crumpled him to the dirt. He tried to crawl as I kicked him and shouted things from my heart to his I cannot remember. Christy hollered for me to stop in the background.

I guess a neighbor called the cops. The next thing I know, I was in handcuffs in the back of a squad car with Elias hoisted into an ambulance on a stretcher. I did not realize how badly I had beat him until it was over.

I served six of nine months for that. Elias was out of the hospital in two. I lost the MMA school we used to run together and my family. My life would never be the same.

CHAPTER 16

FOOD

THE NEXT DAY dawned quickly. Twenty armed soldiers walked the corridor separating our cells, banging the ends of their M-4s along the bars as they went. I knew their types: wanna-be tough guys hiding behind barrels and loaded magazines.

"On your feet," said Captain Warwick. "Grab the bars. Rise and shine. Time to grub. Once in the mess hall, you will keep your mouths shut, or you will not eat."

He signaled, and a loud clanking sent the cell doors opening in sync. Kat and Haley were the first out, Elias and I a close second. The others followed. They were all hungry to eat and implement our game plan.

16-2
THE SMELL OF BREAD

We made our way through the corridors in a single file line at gunpoint. Five soldiers led the group with Captain Warwick at point. Fifteen or so others took the rear. There was no escaping.

Each step was a mental note taken. I had to remember every surveillance camera and doorway if our plan was to work. I doubted it would, but we had to try, and I was counting cameras the way a crackhead at a casino does remaining cash.

Captain Warwick and his dickheads led us down a series of corridors like cattle through a cattle grid awaiting their slaughter. It was worse than war and even worse than being a P.O.W. These were supposed to be my people.

"At least I know what tyranny feels like," I said.

"Whoever said that needs to think about the others in the group before they open their mouth again." Captain Warwick never broke stride or turned back as he talked. "Watching is worse than dying. Trust me on this."

We turned a corner, and the smell of fresh-baked bread traced its way through my nostrils. It was intoxicating. I could only imagine how the others felt. Some of them had been there for nearly a week before my arrival.

The door it was coming from was to our left and just a few paces ahead.

"Time to eat," said Captain Warwick.

The soldiers ushered our watering mouths into the mess hall. I was hungry myself but not starving yet. I had a few days left in me. Desert hungry was not just an expression of war; it was something in which I had first-hand experienced its misery.

16-3
THE MESS HALL

Four soldiers armed at our flanks maintained close positions. The remaining ones departed after the escort was complete. I wondered where they went and what else was in the so-called tower.

"Continue single file," said Captain Warwick. "Get your food and head to the seating area."

"You mean you're actually going to feed us?" asked Anthony.

"Just eat and shut up."

Anthony turned to me. "Mothafuckas ain't fed us since I got here five days—"

He buckled when Captain Warwick motioned one of the soldiers the strike him in the hamstring with the butt of his rifle. Anthony turned to face the soldier when he stood and said nothing. His lips curled and his brow furled, but he kept quiet as he turned to follow the line leading to the trays.

Captain Warwick turned to face me. "You'll learn just as he did. Nothing I say in here is an option, Kemp."

Kemp. I never had a problem with my last name, but I hated it coming from his mouth. The way it rolled off his lips disgusted me, but what could I do but jump the gun on our game plan and ruin it? He was in control in that place, and I hated that too. I was wise enough to follow the others in grabbing a tray and remaining patient. My chance at his neck would come.

All the fighters grabbed trays and plates. Some of the others did not feel like eating, but it is not like they had an option. I was going to eat. I would soon need energy for things to come.

Elias and I reached the soldiers dishing food onto our plates behind stainless-steel cafeteria tables. We guided our trays along its surface until we reached him to receive half a biscuit.

"You're kidding me, right?" asked Elias.

A smirk from the serving soldier was all he got. I knew it was coming. So did Elias. We had spent the last few minutes watching the others' disappointed faces as he set half-biscuits on their plates as well. It was annoying all the same.

We headed to the seating area as instructed. The others followed suit. Romulo, Reece, me, Elias, and Kat sat at one table; Keith, David, and Roger—the quiet one that barely spoke—sat at another. Draven, Anthony, and Haley sat with Brixton's weird-ass and Jean.

"We only get half a biscuit," whispered Reece, "and it tastes like shit."

"Give it to me," said Romulo.

"Hell no. I'm fuckin starving."

"Shut up," I interjected. "Stay sharp."

My hands were hurting, and I clenched my fist to move blood through them. I realized veins darkening and becoming more vascular in them. That is when I decided to put it into action, our plan that is.

"You really are a piece of shit, aren't you?" I roared. "Who fucks their own brother's wife?"

"Damn, bro," said Elias. "You have to start it that way?"

The soldiers took notice.

"Hey," shouted Captain Warwick. "Quiet over there, unless you're done eating."

"Big bad Archer," Elias kept it going. "Who treats their little brother like trash?"

"Hey," said Kat. "Chill."

"I don't know," I answered. "Maybe big brothers who have little brothers that act like white trash?"

Elias stood and tossed his tray across the table at me. "Fuck you."

I retaliated, diving over it and taking Elias down. Chatter amongst the others ensued as the soldiers advanced on us.

"Hey," shouted Captain Warwick. "Cut that shit out."

I was on top of Elias. We ignored the soldiers and were still going at it as they moved in. I cracked him in the face hard enough to send blood pouring from his eye. It had to come across as believable. Besides, I had been looking for an excuse to bleed the little prick for a long time.

I threw a few more punches as he evaded in what we call a guard position: Elias had his legs wrapped around me to immobilize my movements, leaving him in a position for various counters if I got careless. But I rarely got careless.

It was believable and damned near a real fight. Captain Warwick reacted quickly and led the other soldiers towards the action, raising his weapon to strike me. That is when we moved to phase two.

"Now!" shouted Elias.

I turned my attack on Captain Warwick and blocked the oncoming weapon before picking him up and dropping him on his empty head. It rendered him unconscious. Elias popped to his feet while I grabbed Captain Warwick's weapon, but I did not keep it. I tossed it to Elias. He caught it just in time to hit an approaching soldier across the head with it like a baseball bat. A homerun as far as knockouts are concerned.

I rushed another nearby soldier who was readying his weapon to fire. He was not fast enough, not against me. He was too distracted by my little brother holding the gun on him. Had he been a product of war, perhaps he would have gotten me.

I scanned the mess hall while closing the distance and taking the rifle from him—candy from a baby. A few more soldiers entered the mess hall with weapons drawn, and the other prisoners joined the fight by attacking them in unison.

Kat kicked the chunkier one at my left in the head and continued whacking him on the ground while Draven smashed several others in the face with a lunch tray. I watched on as they continued.

Soldiers are never expecting an ambush in calm settings. It was perfect.

Haley was the only fighter there who was mean in spirit like I was. The girl was small, but fuck me if it mattered. She stabbed one of the soldiers in his back with a fork, a lot. Then the little bitch took him down with the fork still in him and kept stabbing.

The room grew quiet once the other prisoners subdued the soldiers. That is what happens when you abduct several of the baddest mother fuckers on the planet and put them in a room together.

The other fighters had turned their attention to me and the soldier lying dead in front of me with Haley's fork still stuck in his mouth. Prong holes in sets of four riddled his neck and face above a pool of blood thick enough to swim in. It was almost laughable. She would have made a great merc.

I bent down and took the key-fob from Captain

Warwick's unconscious pocket and turned to the others. "Grab a weapon. Arm yourselves. Anything you can find."

The others gathered what weapons they could. It was clear that a few did not know how to use them. I demonstrated, but it was the wrong time for half-ass firearm training.

"To check your ammo," I said, "depress this button with your thumb to release the magazine but don't drop it. To reinsert it, pop it back in and give it a hard tap to lock it in like this." I demonstrated. "Make sure your safety's off. That is here. Red their dead. Black, you're jacked. Let's move."

We ran through a concrete and steel corridor leading anywhere but where we were. Elias, Kat, and Haley were at point with me until we reached the door at the end of it. I used the key-fob Captain Warwick was kind enough to share when we got to a locked gate at the corridor's end. It unlocked and cracked open.

CHAPTER 17

HUNGRY FIGHTERS

THE DOOR LED to negative nostalgia. The yard was on the other side of it. I would have chosen another path if I had known, but I did not. I was still waking the morning soldiers walked me to it for my beatdown, which was not the fondest memory, and I failed to pay attention.

We had to enter. Turning back was not an option. Guards were talking somewhere behind us and growing closer.

"Hold up." I scanned for soldiers.

Sniper towers were empty. It was time to discover an exit or take over something besides our cell block—one of the other and whichever came first.

"Okay, I said. "Let's find a way out of this shithole."

We entered the sizable dirt-covered yard cornered by

four sniper towers. There was a large table with food and drinks on it across the way, most likely poisoned with something that would kill or sedate us. My imagination was not strong enough to understand why it was there. Another sick game? No clue, but there is no way he could have known we were going to be there.

It was a tempting lunch, but I had already gambled by eating half of a biscuit in the mess hall and figured giving us such tiny servings was a move to keep us weak yet alive.

"Spread out," I said. "Look for anything."

"For what?" asked Haley. "There's nothing but high concrete walls here."

"Hidden doors," said Elias. "I know there's not a snowball's chance in hell, but we got to try."

"I'll check those sniper tower doors at their base," said Romulo.

The others split up and scoured the large open-topped yard's edge for doors or possible ways out. Like myself, I am sure they knew it was a fruitless hunt. We were as trapped there as we were in our cells.

I moved to the food table in the middle of the yard with Anthony, Jean, and Draven until we were close and stopped. There had to be a way out. I looked to see if anyone was having any luck.

Kat was still combing one of the yard's high walls to find nothing. "There's got to be something."

I approached the large table and moved to grab an oatmeal cookie out of curiosity without being dumb enough to follow through with the urge to take a bite. General Shephard had coated its top with food—a feast fit for a king. Every tasty thing a starving fighter could wish for was present: lobster and butter, roasted chicken, mashed potatoes, hamburgers, fries, lasagna, sausages, fresh-baked bread, hot sauce, three different pies—in which I recognized only one of as key-lime, and more.

"You hungry as I am, big man?" asked Anthony.

"Yeah," I answered, "but I'm not eating it; this could be a cookie poisoned for all we know."

I turned back to see my little brother jump in the center of the yard a few times.

"Feels different here." Elias jumped again. "I swear I hear an echo."

"Check this out," said Anthony.

Elias walked towards the table of food. "Saw it from over there."

"And you didn't come over?"

"I ain't eating that shit."

"See," I said. "Told you it was a bad idea."

"Well…" Elias paused. "Maybe I'll have just a bite."

"No. You're not."

There were only two seats, and they were at opposite ends of the large table with plates, silverware, and empty glasses in front of them.

"Damn," said Elias. "Someone's eating well."

"Yeah," I said. "Don't alert the others."

"Why not?" Elias reached for a burger.

I grabbed his wrist. "Because it could be poisoned or something."

"We're not in a war, Archer."

Soldiers flooded the door we entered the yard through. Lieutenant Brice eased in behind them.

"Still think we're not in a war?" I turned to Elias.

He sighed. "My perspective's changing."

The other fighters turned their weapons towards the entering soldiers. It forced a stalemate. Maybe we were all about to die?

"Drop your weapons," said Lieutenant Brice.

Thirty or more soldiers filled the scene, and they were heavily armed—as usual. An entire platoon had been hiding within the walls of the building. Their guns drew as they corralled us back-to-back at the center of the yard.

"I'd do it sooner than later," continued Lieutenant Brice.

The other fighters lowered their weapons.

"You too, Kemp," he said.

My finger squeezed on the trigger until teeter-tottering on the brink of dropping the hammer and me shooting him right between the eyes—blowing all 36 of his combined I.Q. points out the back of his head.

He pointed to one of the soldiers. "Let him know we're not here to play his games."

The soldier fired a quick round at Kat's feet. She jumped and let out a startled scream, shaking as she looked my way. Nobody on our side of the yard wanted to see her die.

I paused and tensed my trigger finger for that final tug before turning to the other fighters. A few shook their heads slyly as if the soldiers could not already sense their fear. They wanted me to drop the weapon.

"Come on, Archer," said Elias.

I turned back to Lieutenant Brice. He knew enough about me to hold no doubts I wanted to pull the trigger. I was positive General Shepherd had told him a story or three.

"You really want all their deaths on your hands?" he asked.

"Archer," pleaded Kat.

I read her expression. She was not ready to die.

"Please…" she said.

I was sweating as I read the fear in her eyes. I knew what I had to do, but I did not want any part of that damn place. I was ready to be done with it one way or the other.

"Well?" asked Brice. "What's it going to be?"

I took a disappointed breath and lowered the rifle before dropping it to the ground and placing my hands on my head—the misery of living as a captive a second time in my life since Desert Storm was haunting me for another day.

"Good call."

Lieutenant Brice signaled a few soldiers to collect weapons as General Shepherd walked into the yard from the only known entrance. He strolled casually to the large table of food after his goons ushered us 20 paces away from it. Lieutenant Brice moved towards him and took place at his side.

"Where did you think you were going?" asked General Shepherd. "There's nowhere to run."

I cut my head to the table of food. "You eat like kings while you starve these people?"

"No, actually. This was set up for a different reason."

"What's that?"

"I wanted to demonstrate how you'd all be fed here at The Tower. What you just had in the mess hall represents how much and how often you will eat if a single one of you is disruptive. This table here is to inform you of how you could eat every day, so long as there are no incidents. I was even going to let everyone have their share of it today after you left the mess hall."

"Was?" asked Kat.

"Was is correct. One of my men is dead. I can't allow that to go unpunished. Only one of you will eat here today."

General Shepherd eased towards us. "Anthony…"

"Hell yeah."Anthony moved towards the table of food.

"Not so fast," said General Shepherd. "I wasn't finished. Anthony and..."

He paused over his next selection as Anthony swallowed hard, eyeing the food. The man was hungry and hurting over it.

"Uhmmm…" continued General Shepherd,

"Anthony and Jean Bean. You two will fight. Last man standing will join me for breakfast and gets to live."

"Why them?" asked Reece.

"Because they've been here the longest."

"We're not animals," I said.

"I wholeheartedly disagree," said General Shepherd. "That's exactly what you are. What we all are. The only difference between animals and humans is fear of consequence. For some, it's God; for others, it's the law of the land. But once that fear has been removed, our most basic animal instincts always prevail. Rioting. Looting. Killing. Google it if you make it through this, and if I let you out of here."

Jean stepped forward and looked over the table. "I'm in. Let's do it."

"Jean..." said Brixton.

"And in he walks," said General Shepherd, smiling at Anthony as he continued. "Are you ready?"

Jean was already weak. Anthony said he had been there a week longer than he had. He was about to get lucky or hurt. Either way, Anthony flipped his middle finger to General Shepherd and stepped forward.

Draven grabbed his arm. "Don't."

Anthony yanked his arm away. "Been nearly a week since I ate."

He moved to meet Jean at the center of the yard. General Shepherd turned the chair at the end of the table to face the fight and took a seat, smiling and tapping his fingers together in anticipation.

"Alright, gentlemen," said General Shepherd. "Entertain me, and don't hold back. You'll be dead before the fight's over if you do."

Anthony cut him an uneasy eye but dug his feet into the dirt to secure his footing nonetheless. The man was hungry. Starving. His opponent was desperate.

Jean attacked without warning. He was quick for his size, but Anthony covered well as Jean threw a barrage that dropped him. Anthony hit the ground hard without reaching out to catch himself or break his fall: a sign that he was heavily stunned.

Jean rushed to the ground to finish the fight and caught him with a knee as he tried to get up, knocking Anthony to his back again. That is when Jean backed away, thinking Anthony was out. It was a big mistake, one I would have never made.

Anthony rose.

The two warriors went hell inside four walls upon each other for a minute. They were trading shots, applying sweeps, exchanging positions on the ground in a mad scramble, and even getting back to their feet for all of two seconds at one point. That is when it got bad.

Anthony grabbed Jean up and drove him into the ground before placing a shin across Jean's stomach—a position called knee on abdomen—and rained down a barrage of punches to the weakened man's face. Blood flowed freely. His head was bouncing off the ground with every shot: a sign that Jean was more striker than a grappler. An expert ground fighter would have kept his head on the dirt to prevent his head from whipping and jarring the brain upon impact.

It was scary and sad to watch. Haley teared up. Good men were already turning savage.

Draven took a step forward. “Stop.”

Anthony continued raining punches on Jean.

“Anthony,” shouted Draven. “Stop.”

Draven rushed in to tackle him off. They hit the dirt, and Anthony rolled him off to get back on Jean. It was hunger. It was desperation. It was primal.

“It’s over.” Draven pulled at him. “Chill.”

Anthony was not stopping.

“Chill…” Draven strained. “Bro...”

They wrestled for a bit before Anthony stopped.

“Fuck,” said Draven, helping him back to his feet and shaking his head. “He didn’t say you had to kill him, bro.”

Projectiles from a taser sent Draven’s body into random convulsions. He dropped to the dirt.

Anthony snatched the attached taser wires from Draven’s skin. “Fuck’s wrong with you people?”

“That wasn’t Draven’s call to make.” General Shepherd turned to Captain Warwick. “Take them to the chamber. I’m not done with them yet.”

“Bad pick, General,” I said.

“Excuse me?” asked General Shepherd.

“I shot your man. Take me.”

“Leaders make decisions that others pay for, Kemp.” General Shepherd looked at Jean and back to me. “That is how it works." He waved his hand to Captain Warrick. "Take Draven with them. Everyone else, back to your cells. You're all about to learn a valuable lesson."

Guards took Anthony, Jean, and Draven to whatever the hell the chamber is. It was most likely where they had taken Kat earlier and tortured her. As soon as I could kill the twisted fuck without endangering other people's lives, I would.

Shepherd signaled Brice over. "Put Archer in his brother's cell with him."

Lieutenant Brice nodded and directed the prisoners from the yard. The rest of the soldiers followed behind us with weapons at the back of our skulls.

CHAPTER 18

CELL MATES

THEY GUIDED US back to our cells. Lieutenant Brice was nice enough to lead my brother and me to ours personally. I was stepping into my cell when he stopped me.

"You," Lieutenant Brice pointed to Elias's cell. "Over here."

"Not happening," I said.

He pulled his pistol and pointed it at Elias without taking his eyes off me. "Move."

I hesitated, partially to let my brother know my hate for him had not entirely dissipated and to fuck with the soldier. Both felt good, but I did not want him killed just because he fucked my wife. Not by someone else. So, I moved into his cell. Neither of us was happy about it.

"Now this…" I said. "This fucking sucks."

Brice walked off, smirking as if I gave a damn about his opinion or pulse.

"You can have the bunk," said Elias.

"I'm good on the floor," I answered.

"Come on, bro. You're not exactly in the best shape at the moment."

I did not respond. What would have been the point of small talk? I still loved him, sure. But he stuck his dick in my wife while we were still married, and Christopher walked in to catch them in the act. It was part of the reason my son was going through a troubled period.

It was at that moment I think Christopher lost a little respect for her. Like my brother, he still loved her, but his overall care for her parenting was gone. It led him to become unruly.

"Archer," he continued, "please."

"Elias…" I cut him daggered eyes.

"Fine."

Elias stopped talking. He was nervous, scared like the others, and wanted to be close to the brother he betrayed again. The kid had a lot on his mind.

I scooted to the corner, leaned my back against the cold concrete, and propped my head up to rest. We sat in silence for a good hour.

The sound of sliding metal broke our trance. My head shifted skyward, as did those in the cell across from me. A hole was opening in the corner of every cell in eyesight's ceiling to lower a small monitor on a telescoping arm.

We stood and looked to one another for answers. Then the screen clicked on. Draven was sitting in a chair on the monitor with a black hood covering his face.

"Oh no," said Kat. "That's the same room they had me in."

"This is some next-level bullshit," said Haley.

Draven's hands were cuffed behind his back in the center of the room. A black cloth was over his head as well. A noose around his neck hooked over piping and tied off into the wall. There was barely enough slack in the rope for him to breathe, but we knew he was alive. He made subtle movements to stand tall enough to avoid being hanged to death.

Anthony and Jean were chained to the floor against the walls on opposing sides of the room. Jean's face was the only uncovered—battered and beaten from his fight with Anthony. We watched for what seemed like forever until General Shepherd entered and moved to the two chained to the wall. He approached Anthony, then Draven, and pulled the cloths from their heads.

He mused for a moment and turned to face the camera while kicking the chair out from under him. Draven's body tensed through a gurgling choke. His face rushed red.

Haley turned away.

"No…" shouted Kat.

The others in cells around me had similar reactions; things like *Motherfucker's*, *oh-my-god*, and calls to *Draven*—as if he could hear them—slipped from their mouths.

I watched with numbing anger as Anthony stretched his legs out and fumbled to upright the chair with his feet. It dropped twice before he got it upright and kicked it under Draven enough for him to gain footing and avoid choking.

We all had different reactions. My imprisoned friends were worried about our captured colleagues. I was too, but not as much as I was pissed. Something was a little off about me at the same time. A new persona was bottling itself up inside to hide from me, yet I was further serene internally.

General Shepherd signaled Captain Warwick. "Tighten the slack."

Captain Warwick complied, pulling the rope tighter and forcing Draven to stand on his toes for even the smallest breaths. He was exhausted from whatever the hell they had been doing to him before the monitors lowered and came to life for us to watch.

"These people are fucking sick," said Brixton.

General Shepherd drew his pistol from its holster and ejected the magazine. "There's one in the chamber." He walked to Draven and shoved it in the front of his pants. "Count the soldiers around you. There are five of us in here, all armed." He turned to Captain Warwick. "Let him down."

Captain Warwick let up on the slack and motioned a soldier to assist him from the chair. Draven was standing on the concrete shortly after. He was sweating from his momentary struggle to breathe as they uncuffed him.

"You two," said Captain Warwick, "On your feet."

Anthony and Jean stood but remained chained to the wall.

"There's still a balance due for the man I lost," said General Shepherd. "Now, the good news is that we have options. The bad news is… Well, someone's about to die."

He paused to pace as we watched helplessly through the monitor's feed.

"Option one, Draven," he continued, "you could take that bullet and shoot me, but then Captain Warwick and the soldiers in here…they'd likely kill all three of you. Option two, you could kill yourself. Blow your pretty little face off. Game over. Not the worst idea, considering the overall gravity of the situation you're in. And there's option three. This is an interesting one. If I were in your shoes, it would be a no-brainer for me."

He laughed as he paced, pointing and shaking his finger at nothing.

"You're going to love this one," he said. "R.I.P. one of the two other gentlemen in here with you. Your choice. I don't care who you pick, but you and the one you choose get to head back to your cells with the weak link eliminated and a debt paid in full."

Elias pointed to the screen. "Is this guy serious?"

"You're a certifiable nutcase," said Draven. "You know that, right? You're out of your fucking gord if you think I'm killing anyone."

"There is another option," said General Shepherd,

"I can put a projectile between your eyes and call it a day. I'm okay with that as well. You have twenty seconds to make your choice. I suggest you think quickly. The clock is ticking."

Shepherd turned the dial timer on his military watch as Draven took the gun from his pants and pointed it at Shepherd. He did not flinch.

"Shoot him," said Jean. "Shoot that prick."

"Great men act greatly under pressure, Mr. Draven," said General Shepherd. "What kind of man are you? Pull the trigger. You have ten seconds."

Captain Warwick pointed his weapon at Draven. Anthony watched from the other side of the room as Draven put the gun in his mouth. Finger on the trigger.

"D," said Anthony, "listen, brother. Point it over here. It's okay. I'm not afraid."

"Five seconds," counted General Shepherd. "What are you made of? Moment of truth."

Draven took the gun from his mouth and pointed it at Shepherd. I wanted him to pull the trigger. We all did. But it was not that simple, not from where Draven was standing.

"Shoot him," called Jean.

"Stop," said Draven. "Please…I don't wanna kill anyone."

"At me, brother," said Anthony. "This way."

Captain Warwick readied his weapon to fire.

"Time's about up," said General Shepherd. "Three… two... one…"

Draven turned his aim with a swift, sharp flick.

BANG.

Jean's body hit the ground. The others turned their eyes for a moment as he fell. I did not. I needed it to sink in—fuel for the fire.

Draven dropped the smoking gun. It fell to the floor as motionless as the man he had just killed, whose body now lay in a rush of puddling red. Draven was weeping by the time General Shepherd walked to his side, retrieved the pistol, popped the magazine back in, chambered a round, and holstered it.

"You're welcome," whispered General Shepherd. "Now you know who you really are. Escort these two men back to their cells."

"Yes, sir," said Captain Warwick.

Overhead monitors rose back into the cell ceilings, and their sliding paneling closed to conceal them. Sad faces filled our prison holds. All we could do was wait.

CHAPTER 19

DRAVEN'S WALK

WE WAITED FOR Anthony and Draven to return with the soldiers. It was excruciating. We wanted them to be okay but could not bear the thought of seeing the results of what had happened to them. And Draven, I was unsure how he would handle pulling the trigger on an innocent man.

"What do you think happened to them?" asked Haley.

"I don't know," answered Kat. "Let's just hope they're on their way here. Let's just hope they're alive."

A door opened in the distance, and everyone moved to the bars for a better look. We could not see them but hoped they would come into view soon. If the soldiers came alone, they would not be returning if I could get my hands on them.

"Pick up the pace," said an unseen soldier.

The others backed away from the bars when they came into view. Their strides were weighted, Draven's worse than Anthony's. Broken men were taking broken steps.

Anthony kept his chin up. He was suppressing it, but I think most of his inner struggles—if he had any—stemmed from how he envisioned Draven was feeling. He would have died in the room instead of Jean to take the pressure of making that choice from him.

Draven was not dealing with it well. His head hung low. He did not need to be whimpering for us to know he was crying inside. His hands were still shaking, and small splatters of blood decorated the right sides of his face and arm.

Two soldiers—one tall, one short—opened their cell and their captives entered without causing a scene, or a word said. It locked. The shorter of the two smiled at me as he strolled by. I watched him for a moment before lunging out with my right arm for his throat, but he was an inch beyond reach.

He jumped and released a short-lived yell like the little bitch I thought he was.

"Fuck me," he said.

The taller soldier laughed. "Don't act like they didn't warn you about that one."

"I know, but…" He stopped and turned to face me.

Cell bars pushed into bones beneath my fingers' and pained my palms as I crushed down on them. He raised his rifle, and its crosshairs centered on my face. I eased to the bars to give him a better shot.

"Bad idea." The taller soldier eased over and raised his barrel. "Shepherd would kill you."

The shorter soldier remained glued to me. "Look at his eyes."

"Who gives a…" The taller soldier paused for a second, then tugged at the other soldier's jacket. "Come on. Let's go."

He kept his eyes on me for the first few steps as he departed. General Shepherd must have told him something about what they did to me that freaked him out. I shrugged it off. There was nothing to eat, no way to escape, and nothing to do besides talking to Elias, and that was not going to happen.

I laid on the cold concrete to let time slip by.

CHAPTER 20
CONFRONTING ELIAS

THE CELLBLOCK WAS quiet. I laid on the floor and stared at the ceiling for what had to be hours and thought about all that had happened with Draven, Anthony, and Jean, who was no longer with us.

It was the quietest I had heard the cells. The fight and Jean's death were a crushing blow to aspirations for escape and an even bigger hit to our optimism. Recovering from it would take the group time.

My little brother was fidgeting a little and trying to conceal it. I wanted to get up and slap him for it, but I did not. He kept looking my way from the corner of his eye, and it was beginning to annoy the shit out of me.

Elias turned to face me but did not look me in the eyes. "Can we talk about what happened between us?"

"No," I answered. "Save your breath. I don't need to hear anything you have to say. Not right now."

"What I did was unforgivable." He looked up and searched my eyes. "I know that."

I said nothing, not at first. After watching Jean take his final breath in that damn video feed, it felt selfish to think about such things.

"Archer?" he pressed. "Honestly, I just… I'm trying to say I'm sorry for the hundredth time. I really am."

"You're sorry because you screwed her? Or sorry because my son walked in at nine years old and caught you screwing her?"

"All of it." Elias lowered his head. "I'll never forget the look on his face. He was so hurt. So disappointed. It crushed me. And not just that, but the thought of you finding out."

"You destroyed my family, Elias. Took my son from me. Took my life. I lost my will to fight. I lost everything. Right now, Christopher's imploding. I'm lying in a goddamn prison cell, who knows where in the fucking world, with you, and just watched a few guys we both know being forced to kill each other. And this is what you want to talk about? Seriously? Are you fucking stupid?"

"I might be dead tomorrow for all I know," said Elias. "Or you. Or both of us. If I don't do this now, I may not get the chance."

"Still not the time, Elias."

"You were gone for—"

"Goddamn, you're selfish. Ain't life a bitch."

"You were overseas, Archer, for a long time. I was just trying to be there. Trying to help."

I laughed, the first honest one in a long time. I could not believe the little fucker was trying to justify what they had done to Christopher and me.

"Ahh." I continued laughing. "Good looking out, baby bro."

"See?" Elias pointed at me. "There it is. I was always just your little brother. Nothing more. That night we were drinking more than we should have. She came on to me. I was jealous of you. You had it all. I just wanted to see what it felt like for once to be you."

"Well, how'd it feel?" I asked.

"Listen, I was drunk off my—"

I ripped Elias from his bunk and tossed him to the floor. It was instinctual, pure emotion. It had happened before I even realized what was going on. He would have typically put up a better fight, but I caught him off guard, and he was probably feeling guilty about fucking my wife.

I pinned him beneath me in full mount, straddling his chest as I drew back to punch his head through the concrete and stopped at the last possible second—scared I could kill him if I got started. I had always been aggressive, but something inside me was brewing an unwelcome concoction. I felt new impulses coaxing me to lash out, but they were tamed by a new focus and desire to protect my pride.

"Go on," said Elias. "Do it."

It took me a minute, but I relaxed my fist and lowered my arm. My posture shifted as I battled the unexpected desires to kill and protect. I would have beaten Elias's ass before they injected me with that red shit.

"Now get off me," he said.

I got off him, but the darkness growing inside me was teaming with the anger I still harbored for him. A few punches to his face would have only made it worse. My head shook. I fell lost to thoughts about what he had done and how we ended up trapped inside The Tower. To top things off, disconnect from my former self was building.

Elias was staring. "Archer?"

"What now?" I asked,

"What's wrong with your eyes?"

"I'm kind of pissed here. What do you think? Shut up for a minute."

"I mean…" He paused to study me. "They look funny. You, okay?"

"Elias…"

"No." He leaned in for a closer look. "I'm being serious. They have a golden color. Bright. I don't know what you call it, but the white part of your eye isn't… I mean, they look like cat or lion—"

"On your feet, Archer," said an unwelcome voice.

Elias and I turned our attention to the bars.

Lieutenant Brice approached with two other soldiers. He opened the cell and drew his weapon like he was itching to fire it. "General Shepherd wants to see you."

I stepped out cautiously. The soldier at my right, the uglier of the two, went to shut the cell door, but Elias was holding it open.

"Where are you taking him?" asked Elias.

He got the killing end of an M-4 pressed into his forehead for caring. His eyes moved back and forth between the soldier and me as he eased away with the barrel holding its position against his skin.

"It's okay," I said. "It'll be all right."

Elias knew I did not believe it any more than he or anyone else did, but he eased away so the soldier could lock him in. They handcuffed me and dropped a black hood over my head as they had with Draven. I could only imagine what Elias was thinking, but I assumed it was the same thing I was—*Jean's fate would soon be upon me.*

CHAPTER 21

WALKING BLIND

WE WALKED FOR at least 15 minutes. I think it was more to disorient me than anything else. Though I had been black-bagged, they gave me no chance to memorize the twists and turns of The Tower's layout. No one spoke either. They simply guided me with hands clamped tightly around my upper arms.

There were doors. Some were lock and key; others were either key coded or required a badge. One was a combination of the two. There was also a set of steps I almost tripped over. Bastards could have warned me to step up. I am positive it was intentional.

An elevator released a ding, and we entered, sending my stomach into an unpleasant drop as it accelerated rapidly skyward. There was no muzak to soothe the ears. We waited for it to stop, ding, and allow us to exit.

They led me down another couple of halls, or corridors, or whatever the hell they were in that twisted place. What did not make sense was the fact that we got on another elevator to head back down. They were keeping me confused.

We exited when it stopped and marched forty paces before they opened another door and ushered me in.

21-2
BURNING CEDAR

They uncuffed me. Backsides of both my eyes stung under bright lights when a soldier pulled that black cloth from my head. I was glad he took it off. I like using my eyes, and it was hard to breathe under it; I was not surprised to find General Shepherd in front of me.

He was seated on top of his desk and pointed to a liquor-stocked wet bar across the plush office: stained oak swirled with inlays of marble, gold trim, and lights you might find in an upscale nightclub. The carpet was a welcoming soft, plush red contrasting with the cold concrete flooring of our cells.

Lieutenant Brice took a position to cover the exit.

"Can I get you something?" asked General Shepherd.

"What do you want?"

"Have a drink. Some of these bottles are fifty-plus thousand dollars." He smiled. "I know you're a drinking man these days."

I did not answer, and I was not about to play his games.

"Okay then." He pulled out a black box, removed a small piece of cedar, lit it, and used it to light the only cigar in the box. I snickered at his desire to present himself as powerful while he turned on an overhead ventilation system. It quickly cleared the room of any signs of smoke.

"Have a seat," he said.

"I'll stand," I replied.

"Suit yourself. How are you feeling? You look much better. Hell of a beating you took out there."

"What do you want?"

"I just wanted to help you." He took a puff of the cigar. "You're a soldier at heart. One of the best. Wanted to help you find yourself again, make you stronger, and get you back serving to your country."

"Here's the deal." I took a step towards him. "Let my brother go, and you can do whatever you want with me."

"That's a generous offer, Archer. It is. But I can already do whatever I want with you. I thought that'd be obvious by now."

I knew he was not going to listen. So, I stayed quiet—no use in talking to a wall.

"Plans have changed," continued General Shepherd. "I'll be making an announcement this evening. Big day tomorrow. There's no turning back on this one for either of us. The stakes are too high. You take care of yourself, son."

"That's all you brought me up here for?" I asked. "What was the point?"

"Just wanted to tell you good luck in person," he answered. "Figure I at least owe you that. Good luck tomorrow, Archer. And you're welcome."

"For what?"

"For what we did to you."

General Shepherd turned his back to me and poured himself a drink while Lieutenant Brice and the soldiers put that shit-smelling cloth back over my head, cuffed me, and escorted me from the office. The path back was the same, dark, crooked way they had walked me last time.

I knew General Shepherd did not care. He had brought me up there to clear a spec of his moral conscious, probably the last one he had. I only had one thing on my mind when I walked in darkness back to my cell: *Fuck him if he thinks he's breaking me.*

CHAPTER 22

THE FLY

THEY UNBAGGED ME as soon as we got back to the cell. My eyes took a moment to adjust again, but I think I was getting used to the sudden change in lighting. It did not take as long as before.

Elias was pacing anxiously in his cell when I returned. He was worried about me and approached the bars as I neared with escorting soldiers. He sighed relief, most likely expecting me to be fucked up and half-dead again.

One of the soldiers opened the cell and uncuffed me. "There you go."

"Want me to put that gun on your hip to your head and pull the trigger for you?" I asked.

"Just get in your cell, Kemp."

I walked in and sat on the cot, waiting for them to

leave so I could drown the urge to break small bones in their necks, but they stuck around for a few minutes talking outside our cage about their dinners the night before. The rest of us had not eaten for shit. I knew what they were doing, but I ignored them until they left.

"What happened?" asked Elias.

My veins were hurting more than they had before and felt to be flaring up. I had been trying to ignore it, but it was getting difficult. They were getting darker. My hands were worse. I traced them to my fingertips while Elias watched me.

Once white nails were black as if I had slammed in a car door. A raised thumbnail caught my attention. I tilted my head and picked at it, barely making contact before it slipped off my finger fell to the floor. The damn thing just came loose as if it were waiting for a breeze to release it.

I felt like Jeff Goldblum's character must have in *The Fly*.

"The fuck's happening to you?" asked Elias.

He leaned in for a look and turned slowly back to my hand. Another nail was growing in its place. It was thicker, longer, and had a slight point.

I leaned against the wall. Something about me was shifting. Explaining it was beyond my ability, but something inside me—both physically and psychologically—had been altered by Dr. Kepler the day they put that red shit into my bloodstream.

"Archer?" asked Elias.

The P.A. system came to life again. "Good evening. This is General Shepherd. Duct taped to the bottom of your cots is a nice, shiny, brand new, tactical compression uniform to replace the not so pretty orange ones you're currently wearing."

Elias, Kat, Anthony, Haley, Draven… Everyone searched. Each of us had a pair folded up and taped to the underside of our cots.

"Now we're playing dress-up for this guy?" asked Haley. "You've got to be fucking kidding me."

We knew he expected us to wear them, but I figured they were laced with something. I held no wants to put it on.

"I expect all of you to be wearing them before we convene in the yard," said General Shepherd.

I reached for the uniform, examined it, and looked at the others. It was the same as my little brother's appointed attire and the two in the cell across from us. He had pinned a note to mine. I recognized his handwriting.

'CURTESY OF GENERAL SHEPHERD'

Fucker was taunting me.

Kat was already naked and pulling the earth-toned tactical compression uniform over her body. It molded itself around every curve. She was hard not to look at, but I was far from interested. She and Elias already dated in the past, and I was not the backstabbing asshole my brother was.

"You're to put yours on as well, Kemp," said General Shepherd.

I turned to the nearest camera and flipped him a bird capped with a sharp nail, but I put it on. Getting the others in more trouble or killed was not something I wanted on my hands. I cared for them—at least I was starting to—more than usual. It left me wondering how much I would change mentally and physically before the red serum ceased its dance within me.

"Use this time to prepare your minds for the challenges to come," continued General Shepherd, "and I can assure you it will be challenging."

I finished putting on the uniform. It was tight but custom-tailored to my frame. It flowed with me.

Five minutes later and we were greeted with a dozen soldiers. Captain Warwick and Lieutenant Brice were with them. A few moved to open our cells. Others remained in the hallway at a distance in case any of us behaved stupidly.

"You know where to take them," said Brice.

"Follow us," said the soldiers opening Kat and Haley's cell.

Three soldiers walked in front of us, and we followed as ordered through the recreational room, a few doors, and into a pair of hallways. The last hallway opened twice as tall and wide as the others. A heavily reinforced door stood tall at its end. I recognized it. We were heading to the yard.

A soldier halted and turned to face us. "Hold your position."

We stopped.

Another soldier, the one at point, moved to the door and used voice authorization to open it before turning back to us.

"All right," he said, "come on."

That was it, the beginning of the end.

CHAPTER 23

THE SQUARE HOLE

I STEPPED THROUGH THE door and into a furious morning sun peeking between parting clouds and squinted my eyes. It did not bother me as much as the other captives, but it was bright.

"Please note the tables," said General Shepherd over the P.A. "I'll be joining you shortly."

"Joining us for what?" I wondered, staring at the empty tables.

I guess he wanted us to sit in the sun and wait. And that's what we did. 30 or more minutes passed. Luckily for us, the clouds showed mercy.

We gathered in small groups, knowing we were about to be tested. Some were training to warm their joints while others stretched. Soldiers surrounded us in vast numbers at the yard's outskirts.

I was alone wrapping my wrists and studying those new nails of mine with hopes of eventually burying them into General Shepherd's jugular vein. They were growing and getting sharp. I had an urge to grind them against a hard surface.

Shepherd's voice made me cringe when it echoed the field over the P.A. system again, "Your primary objective is to survive by any means necessary."

Elias was sitting in front of Kat at a corner of the yard, helping her stretch. They were a nice visual match whether they got back together or not, but I often wondered if she knew what he had done to me, or understood why we did not speak, because I never talked about it.

They were talking about something but too far away to hear. My curiosity grew, and I strained to listen. Head cocking. Eyes squinting. The next thing I knew, I could hear them. It surprised me so much that I almost lost my concentration.

"There's gotta be a way outta of this, right?" asked Kat.

"Wish I could make you feel better," answered Elias, "but I don't know. This is bad, Kat."

"I know."

My son approached me in the yard with a cheery smile on his face.

"Christopher?" I asked.

"Yeah," he answered. "Come on. Who else would I be?"

I knew he could not have been there, but part of me believed it to be true. Sure, I talked to him in my head when I was drunk at times, but it had been different the days since Dr. Kepler got ahold of me. I could see and feel him. My mind was playing tricks on me.

"You're not real," I said. "How are you here?"

"I've been here, goofball. I want to tell you a secret."

I glanced to the others as if they could see Christopher, then knelt by his side and tilted my head so he could whisper his secret into my ear, but I could not understand him. His words were stammers of gibberish.

"I… I can't understand you."

Christopher disappeared. I sat in the hot dirt covering the ground. I was angry and confused but knew I needed him as much as he did me.

Kat was staring at me. I could hear and see her from the corner of my eyes.

"What's up with that?" asked Kat.

"He's always done that," answered Elias. "He's a little off since the war, but it's gotten worse since he's been here. I've asked him who he talks to before."

Elias leaned to his side to stretch his back as I listened to their conversation from a distance, one I did not want to and should not have been able to hear. LS8 was already becoming a curse. Whatever that serum was doing to me needed to leave my body. Or stay. It felt good, but I was becoming torn about it.

Regarding what Elias said, he was right. I talked to Christopher often, but I never saw him so vividly as in

The Tower. It was getting hard to tell if he were there or not.

"What did he say?" asked Kat.

"What's that?" Elias asked in return.

"When you asked him who he talks to?"

"Said he's talking to his son."

"Christopher?"

Elias nodded. Additional soldiers filled the yard from the main entrance to split in multiple directions and line the yard's edges to the total capacity. Rifles raised to aim down at us. I thought we were about to be executed.

"What now?" asked Kat.

General Shepherd, Captain Warwick, and Lieutenant Brice stepped through the border of soldiers. It is interesting to see a man standing in front of other men to give the illusion of superiority while simultaneously hiding behind.

"There are three rules that I live by," said General Shepherd. "One: Good men will die. Two: You can't change rule one. And three: You'll die trying to change the first two rules. Sometimes we are tested. Not to show our weaknesses, but to discover our strengths."

Gas hissed. The other prisoners studied the yard in confusion, mumbling amongst themselves.

CHAKANK

It was a deafening sound.

Heavy metal locks were releasing. The dirt ground shook low on the Richter scale but noticeable. Deep, square-shaped lines revealed themselves at the center of the yard. They rose at one end to announce an increasingly larger opening. A giant square was rising from the surface we were standing on.

It raised six inches from the ground before it stopped. The sound of churning gears filled the air as it moved from left to right across the yard. Dirt fell into the newly formed opening as it shifted to the side, and a large square hole was heading down into what might as well have been the depths of hell in the yard's center.

"I knew there was something under there," said Elias.

I stepped forward to peer over its edge. The falling earth had created an unnatural sandstorm enveloping a set of descending steps free of handrails. No one moved. No one breathed until the dust settled.

A soldier handed General Shepherd a microphone, and his voice resonated over the P.A. system. "Make it to the ground floor, and you may just survive this."

The others moved to gather around me, stopping to search one another for answers they would not get.

"What do you think?" asked Elias.

"It's either our path to freedom or a staircase to sit with Satan," answered Kat.

"We need to stick together," I said.

"This is a roof?" asked Reece.

"I guess," answered Haley. "We are on top of this thing."

"Now we know why there are no exits up here," said

David. "I'm headed straight to the bottom. That's the way out. You coming, Haley?"

She gave him a nod before turning to Kat. "You going to come with me?"

"I'm sticking with Archer and Elias," answered Kat. "You should wait too."

Haley, Keith, and David approached the massive opening into the floor ahead and investigated the abyss. Their faces illuminated from an unknown source. Something was glowing or emitting light from below.

Kat looked at Elias and back to Haley, shaking her head to say no but received a sad smile from Haley.

"David," I said, "We should stay together like we did in the mess hall."

"I got this, big dog," said David. "Let's go."

"Fuck it," said Roger, "I'm going with them."

Keith and David stepped towards the hole, laid on their bellies, and slid into it before dropping from sight.

Roger moved to its edge and stood beside Haley. "See you guys at the bottom. I'm out."

He squatted down and jumped. The next thing we knew, we were listening to him bounce off whatever the hell he was supposed to be landing on and screaming, then came a thud followed by a silence that matched his nontalkative nature.

Haley rushed to the edge, looked down, and turned back to us with terror in her eyes. We were hesitant about proceeding after that, but we were not exactly sitting in a chair of alternatives. We could either follow the others or die.

It took less than a minute for General Shephard to remove his sidearm and fire a warning shot. It passed right between Elias and me—burying into the high walls on the other side of us.

Elias jumped and cursed. It was just a warning shot, but I guess it surprised him.

"Wait for us," said Kat.

I turned to see Haley nearing the square hole.

"I'm sorry," said Haley. "I just want out of here."

She eased over the edge and shared a final connection with Kat before easing her legs over the side and dropping in. The rest stayed with me in silence for a moment. We listened for anything and could only assume Haley made it all right.

"The next one won't be a warning shot, boys," said General Shephard.

"We don't know what's down there," I said. "We have to stick together."

The group agreed. None of us knew what was to come, but I learned in life to take point…and that I needed to be the first into the opening.

CHAPTER 24

DESCENSION

A LARGE, GLOWING, GLASS staircase with no hand railing led to a depth three floors below. A matching platform atop it was a solid nine-foot drop.

"What the…?" Elias paused.

"You're going down on your own or falling in." General Shepherd raised his sidearm again. "Your choice."

"I'll go first," I said.

The climb down was tricky from the start. I had to hang from the upper level at the yard's dusty base and drop several feet onto a glowing glass platform. Between cameras lining the yard walls and those encircling our access point, I think someone was hoping to capture a slip and fall. But they had already caught Roger's death on camera if the twisted bitches wanted something to rub one out to later.

The staircase went down three floors. I was not sure how thick it was, but it looked sturdy enough to hold one of us at a time. Its edge glowed red like the end of a fiberoptic cable and acted as the only light source. We could see, but who the hell wants to walk on glass?

The others were peering over the edge. Elias was slinking over behind me. He was about to drop down at my side.

"Hold up," I said.

"What?" He hung over its edge. "Why?"

"I don't know how much this thing can hold. Feels flimsy."

"Okay." Elias's fingers were slipping on the sand-covered overhang. "Would you mind hurrying then?"

I eyed the darkness encompassing the central region of the massive hole. I had to move, but placing my foot onto the glass staircase felt treacherous. Five steps later, I told him to drop, but his hands slipped as I spoke. He nearly tumbled off the side of the platform.

"Elias," shouted Kat.

He hurried from the edge as he stood. "Fuck me."

"You, okay?" I asked.

"I'm good, but this stuff is slick. Be careful when you drop down, Kat."

She was worried, but I was concerned for the others more than myself. At least my balance and reflexes were feeling better than ever.

"Stay five steps apart," I said. "We don't want this shit breaking on us."

They nodded.

24-2
THE GLASS STAIRCASE

Cameras were everywhere. Some of them angled to follow us as the others took turns dropping down and descending. Brixton was the last to land on the top of the glass staircase. I was glad they agreed to spread out. There were too many of us to risk combining our weight to a single area.

The clear stairway lit our bodies with a soft red hue as we descended. I stopped at a secondary platform to glance over the edge again. A few more stories, and we would be on a solid surface. Gazing down for an extended period was a no-no. It was disorienting looking through a transparent surface that worked like a magnifying glass to create multiple depths of field. And, although I did not have basophobia, I understood why some would. Nobody wants to fall unless they jump.

Draven lost his balance halfway down the staircase and fell. He was nearly over the edge when Anthony took a few steps up and caught him wrist to wrist. It was a good thing we had a heavyweight with us.

"Shit," said Draven. "Thanks, bro."

Anthony pulled him back up. "Watch your step."

"Yeah, no shit."

We continued cautiously and reached the bottom intact.

24-3
BEYOND THE STAIRCASE

Cameras lining the ceiling became bright with green lights and illuminated the lowest point of the hole. They did not power up until we stopped in the shadowy base of the staircase. They had switched to night vision. I eased from the staircase base, and Roger's body came into view.

Draven walked over to it. "Why didn't he just ease over like the rest of them?"

"Because he's an idiot," answered Anthony.

I almost laughed. "Read my mind."

We moved through the base of the landing towards an open doorway and entered.

"This would make a great horror film," said Elias.

Nobody responded. I think he said it to distract himself. I am not sure.

An elevator ahead was dimly lit by a control button at its side. Reece, Brixton, and Romulo headed direly to it and pushed the elevator call button, leaving the rest of us alone in the darker area of whatever the hell they called that section of The Tower.

I looked up as they pushed its call button. General Shepherd and other soldiers without valor were lining the overhead entrance as it closed. We had been herded into a trap, and Romulo was having no luck with the elevator.

"Mutha…" said Romulo.

"What?" asked Brixton. "You thought you'd get in and head to the lobby for a drink?"

Brixton walked to his side. "Wanna try the elevator again?"

"Shut up and help me," answered Romulo.

They pulled at the elevator door in an attempt to open it with their hands, but it refused to budge. Their eyes cut to the sign above it:

'10TH FLOOR'

I stepped into the center of the ascension hole and scanned for clues: the walls were bare concrete and steel, the ceilings were low, and there was nothing of use beyond what they had already found—which was nothing beyond cameras and concrete at every turn.

"This way." I motioned the others towards what appeared to be an open door in the dark area across the floor.

We entered the door to find ourselves in a corridor allowing us to move in only one direction, and that was left. Lighting was overly dim, but we could see better light ahead at an upcoming 'T' intersection. We were about to merge with another corridor.

We did not find Haley until making our way to it. She was petrified with wide eyes and hyperventilating breaths. Kat and Elias moved to her side.

"Haley," asked Kat, "are you ok? Where are the others?"

Haley pointed to a door with a flashing red light over it. "They went in there. I was scared."

"We're all scared, honey."

"Believe that," said Elias. "Come on. Stick with us. We'll get through this."

I searched for the best path. There were not many options. Left or right? It did not matter. Both led to dead ends stopping at closed double doors. A red light flashed above the one to our right while another remained a constant glow.

Elias extended a hand. Haley took it so he could help her up. Archer, Draven, and Anthony made their way towards the closed double doors with the solid red light.

Draven kicked them a few times, but they would not open. He looked at the retinal scanner. "Fuckin' coded-ass security bullshit." He kicked it again. "Dammit..."

"We have to go the way the others did," I said.

I moved to the door with a flashing red light and opened it. A dark stairwell awaited us on the other side of it, but it was bright enough on our end to see. Down we went.

24-4
DARK STAIRWELL

We made our way down a cautious descent enveloping us further into darkness. At least it was solid. Walking on a glass staircase is Russian roulette with gravity.

"I can hardly see shit in here," said Brixton.

"I see fine," I said.

"It's your eyes, Archer," said Elias. "That's what I was trying to tell you. Something's—"

"Shhh…" I interrupted. "Hear that?"

"Hear what?"

"I heard something. Anyone else hear it? Thuds or something? Anything?"

They did not hear it. Figures. It was getting harder for the others to peer the dark, but a sign came into view when the steps cut left:

'9TH FLOOR'

I opened the door and led the group into a dimly lit room.

CHAPTER 25

2.0

THE ROOM WAS massive and open. Rows of eight-foot-tall pods an arm's width wide stood sporadically throughout its floors. Smoked glass doors were a constant on each of them; wires protruded from the walls around us to fill a concrete scene with a forest of technology. Mighty pillars held the ceiling-high at bay.

"Eight floors to go," said Kat. "So far, so good?"

A few of the pods brightened from the inside. Their internal lights backlit silhouettes of large humans in each. Red lights with consecutive numbers hung above each pod on long cables.

"Hey…" said Elias. "What's that?"

I did not want to know what had caught his attention, but I moved with him regardless. I figured it would be another one of those men, those things that attacked me in the yard. Perhaps a dozen of them were ready to kill us.

A pair of bodies laid unmoving on the concrete near the pods 40 feet ahead. It was Keith and David. Clothes ripped and bloody. Bones exposed. Something had beaten them bad enough their insides were no longer their insides.

"Oh my God," said Kat.

"Aw, hell no," said Reece. "That is fuckin' ruthless. This shit ain't cool, man. This shit ain't cool."

Elias grabbed him. "Calm down."

"Take your hands off me."

"Quiet," I said. "Both of you."

People die when they lose their cool in war. It might not have been on a battlefield, but it did not need to be. I knew what the others did not—we were in that peaceful moment before the battle.

A loud buzzer went off and startled the others. Red lights over two of the pods were flashing with rhythmic beeps. The smoked-glass fronts rose slowly.

"In formation," I said. "Now."

"Formation?" asked Kat.

"Back-to-back, everyone."

Two figures emerged. One was more significant than the other and hunched forward as it walked calmly towards us. The two pale creatures were almost free of hair. Their exteriors were rough like withered, petrified, wooden remains found in pyramids upon excavation.

Strangely textured skin of the exact nature in darker shades stretched tightly over deeply shredded muscles.

They stopped a few feet away. Dead eyes, strange with a dirty black sclera, peered upon us with emotionless gazes. Dark veins riddled exposed flesh. One of them was missing an eye. Felt like I was looking at a goddamn ghost.

"That's the guy that almost killed me," I said.

"You said he was dead," said Elias.

"He was."

Something about the large man had changed. It was different. Upgraded. Ugly Fucker 2.0. He did not move or blink.

"Why's he just standing there?" asked Haley.

"I don't know," I answered.

"He's not even looking at us. You think he's even aware we're here?"

"He knows."

Brixton eased up to it for a closer look. "I don't think he does. I think he's braindead or something." He circled the large motionless man in examination.

General Shepherd's voice echoed a single word over the P.A.: "Attack."

2.0 palmed Brixton across his face, dropping him like a swatted fly, and snatched him from the floor by the head in a single stroke.

"Brixton," shouted Kat.

The big fucker shook him the way you shake a

chicken to break its neck and dropped his body carelessly to the floor. No way he was alive, not after that.

Haley stepped back. "Oh my God."

"This time you die," it said.

The others attacked eight of them against 2.0 and the other creature. They were doing okay with the second one. It was smaller. But 2.0 was out for blood.

I could feel my brows ruffling. Something was off about my eyes. They itched. My vision swirled, and pain seared in their sockets where they connected to my... To wherever the fuck they were connected. I dropped to the ground in agony while the others fought. A growl escaped. It was something innate, like that of a lion. Then it went away, and—without meaning to—I attacked.

I tackled 2.0 to separate him from the smaller creature, but it tossed me into a pillar. It stung, but it did not at the same time. I surged back at him, clawing strikes with those new nails of mine until 2.0 fell to the hard floor leaking blood, and I was right back on him. Half technical. Half savage.

2.0 turned to stand, but I raked his eyes with an unintentional roar to cut deep. A rear-naked choke followed as the others battled the smaller creature. The beast flailed as I kept an eye on the others. It dropped to the ground, spun, flopped, and was up again with me on its back. Rough skin on his neck pressed ever tighter into my forearms.

I was not trying to choke it. I was trying to kill it.

Dark veins were bulging through my hands and forearms. My teeth clinched to the point of cracking. I squeezed until 2.0's struggle dissipated.

The others were defeating the smaller creature, but I was not letting go of the one that beat my ass in the yard that day. It went limp as I crushed its lifeless neck until a loud crack released.

Elias approached me as the others watched on. "Archer?"

I was losing control. Something else, something not me, was killing that thing. I could not stop. Urges were was more substantial than the will to release my hold.

"Archer?" Elias continued.

A long moment passed before whatever was so angry within me settled. A fantastic calming materialized into me as I released my death grip. Elias eyed me for a bit before extending his hand, but I did not take it.

I stood on my own and walked past him. "Keep moving."

They followed as told to do.

BEEP-BEEP-BEEP.

Lights on the four remaining pod doors were flashing. One of them opened, allowing another of Dr. Kepler and General Shepherd's creations to emerged, step forward, and beat its chest like an ape. Three different innovations of madness with matching temperament emerged from the other pods and approached behind the first.

All four dashed across the open concrete to hurdle

their dead counterparts and attack us. The other fighters teamed up instinctively, two on one against the smaller 2.0 type creatures. Reece and I were together as the battle ensued. The beasts fought us with skill and intelligence. They even showed martial arts intuition. They were more robust than the other fighters, for sure.

Reece landed but a single shot before he was hit with a stiff right hand. He went down after that, and the damn thing stomped on his head before I could move in, crushing it like tank tracks rolling over an ISIS captive.

He was the first killed in the savage exchange and would usually not have been missed. At least, not by me. Part of me felt terrible for some reason. Maybe it was PTSD from losing squad members under my command in the past? Perhaps the serum was altering me more than I thought? It had to be something because I would have been unphased by Reece's death a week ago. Time would tell.

I was left to fight alone. It was fate, not that I believed in such things. But I could move better without Reece getting in my way.

I maintained Kat and Elias in my peripheral as I fought. I wanted to keep an eye on her and my little brother for intuitive reasons. He and I were far from being on the best of terms, but we were coming around.

Kat and Elias were magic together and showed their enemy what made them champions. Elias would bury his shin into its thigh or stomp its knee every time it focused on Kat. When it did not, she would move in and trip it from behind. They had it turning back and forth, unable to land shots, and kept it off-balanced until they dropped it. Then, like I saw him do on the street once, Elias booted it in the face. It would have ended most fights. It was tough, but they handled it.

Elias did get hit once. Stunned him badly, but Kat kept it distracted enough not to finish him off. They killed it by stomping its head while it was on its back, forcing it to bounce off the concrete repeatedly. Payback for Reece, though he was not the most deserving of it.

The one I was fighting had to be angry. I was dancing and taunting around it while it tried to hit me so I could keep my eye on Elias and Kat. It stopped to scream and beat the ground for a moment. It still looked like it was primarily human, but something else had taken over all four of them. It was ape-like in the same way I felt the others to be my pride.

The ape-like man took a mighty shot at me—slow bastard. I ducked, spun behind, took it down, and pushed both my fingers through its eyes to grab the sides of its skull. It gave me the perfect grip to bounce its head off the concrete a few dozen times and left it to lie.

I scanned the others with my thumbs still in the thing's eyes.

Draven and Anthony's attacker became ferocious. It had already knocked Draven down into a drunken state by the time I looked their way. It was also out-wrestling Anthony, who was an Olympic medalist, on a technical level.

Haley and Romulo were not faring well against the other. The beast countered every attack. It might as well have been a machine programmed with all their tendencies and best moves. It stunned Romulo and ripped his arm from his torso.

"Help," screamed Haley.

She tried to defend herself, but the creature had Romulo's arm in hand and beat her with the meaty club. Romulo clutched where his arm once was while bleeding profusely and rolling about on the floor in agony. He was not going to make it, not with that much blood loss, and certainly not down here.

I moved in to grab the creature attacking Haley and dismantled its train of thought by dumping it onto its head. Its neck broke. I like that sound when it echoes from the body of those worthwhile of it.

We continued fighting four on one as Romulo collapsed lifelessly in a pool of his blood behind us. Haley was barely hanging on and struggling to help us kill the last mutation. She had been hurt badly and could not focus well. I could see it in her eyes—that lost feeling you get when you know your body is no longer working right and survival instincts take over.

It was an anvil for its size: slower than the rest, not as intense, but made of proverbial iron. We must have beaten the damn thing for five minutes before it finally fell. We stomped and kicked it, wrestling it back to the ground every time it tried to rise. It caught me with a hard shot, but I took that one for Draven. He was already dazed, and we could not afford to lose him to brain damage; I was already worried about Haley's condition.

We kept it down and hammered the damn thing like it had slain our mothers until we killed it. Our breathing was heavy by the time it was over, proving the battle fast-paced enough to tire a group of pros. I was not looking forward to things to come.

I stood calm, almost emotionless. I didn't feel generally angry inside anymore. Perhaps it was partially working things out with Elias that had done it, but I still thought it was that red shit coursing my body. There was no way to tell, but killing those things felt better than it should have.

The others collected themselves and regrouped back-to-back. Haley wobbled and collapsed to a knee. Then almost to her face.

"I got you." Kat helped her to her feet.

"My head hurts," said Haley.

Elias rushed to Romulo's body and knelt to check his vitals. I watched for a second before he shook his head. Another life lost to The Tower.

I took point without a word. The others studied me as I led them, not that I knew where I was going. The tower was far from mazelike. Its design was sinisterly devised to herd us into further chaos.

We searched for a way out besides where he had entered. That is when I noticed it. The pods the creatures emerged from had closed to their original positions, all except for one. A focused red light illuminated it.

Walls dimmed to a lightless state, then the center of the room darkened to match. The pod lit under a red hue became our attention's focal point. General Shephard had deliberately steered us.

My vision was good in the darkness, better than it had been a few days earlier. However, a few colors were fading from my sight as time passed, mainly leaving shades of blues and greens with hints of others for me to see. The other captives did not need to know about my eyes or what I could see. They were worried enough about me as it was.

I approached the pod to find an opening with a descending ladder inside. I sent the others a hopeful nod for reassurance that we had each other's backs. "We don't separate. I won't leave you; you don't leave each other."

They nodded.

"Archer…" said Anthony. "Your eyes…"

Empty thoughts loomed within me. I did not answer. It was best I proceeded down and stayed at point.

I entered the pod and headed down the ladder. Anthony, Draven, Kat, Elias, then Haley, that is the order they followed.

CHAPTER 26
DIGESTION

WE REACHED THE bottom of the ladder to find it led to an empty concrete room the size of a large walk-in closet. A single door rested on the opposite side of the room.

"I'll go first," I said.

Elias stepped up. "I got it."

I put my hand on his chest to stop him.

"Let Big Man here go first if he wants to," said Anthony. "Shit, don't be eager to die up in this bitch."

"That's comforting, Anthony," said Haley. "Real comforting."

I turned the knob and cracked it enough to peek inside.

"What's that smell?" asked Elias.

I turned to face the others. "Try to control yourself in here."

"What is it?" asked Draven.

I moved in with the rest behind me. It was another room, only larger, and it had something in it. Kat and Elias stared like Adam and Eve lusting over forbidden fruit.

A cherrywood dining table with swirled inlets stood at its center with a mouth-watering display rested atop it: lobster and butter, roasted chicken, mashed potatoes, hamburgers, fries, three different pies, lasagna, sausages, fresh-baked bread, hot sauce, and a few things fancy beyond my palette. It was a mirror image to the one General Shepherd had Anthony and Jean fighting over.

"Damn," said Kat. "That's a lot of food."

"No," said Elias. "This is messed up."

Anthony moved in to grab a hamburger.

Elias stopped him. "Don't eat that."

"Man," said Anthony, "you do you. Let me do me."

"He's right," I said. "Could be poisoned. Or..." I held up my hand to brandish my new nails and dark-tinted veins. "It could be something worse."

He studied me for a moment. I watched as he turned back to the food, thought about it, and took a bite.

"No," said Draven. "Dude, what? Are you—"

"If I'm dead," Anthony interrupted while the mouthful of hamburger, "sick, or look like shit in an hour, you know not to eat any of it."

Draven snickered. "Jesus, dude."

"Why you always bringing Jesus into shit, man?" asked Anthony. "Look. I ain't ate in like a week, done banged with that Jean Bean dude over this, and you had to shoot him before it was over with."

Draven looked away.

"I'm eaten it," Anthony continued. "Plain and simple. We ain't makin it out this shit anyhow." He took another bite.

"That's that," I said. "We'll wait and see how he feels."

Anthony finished his burger. "Might as well have me one of these beers while I'm at it." He grabbed a Samuel Smith's Oatmeal Stout, popped the top off against the edge of the table, and tipped it up. "Dayum, this is some a good ass beer. You want one, D?"

"Nah," answered Draven. "I might get one in an hour or so."

"What happened to ride or die?"

"That's what I'm waiting to find out."

They shared a laugh. The other smiled. I have got to admit it was kind of funny.

"All right, D," said Draven. "I'll feel ya."

I sat against the wall while he reached back in for something else to eat, not paying attention to what he was grabbing.

"Well," said Elias, "Now we play the waiting game."

Elias moved to Kat and took her hand. She smiled as he pulled her to sit against the door for an embrace. He looked my way for a second as Haley and Draven got comfortable. I closed my eyes to save energy.

26-2
GUILT

The forest around us was beautifully lush: Spanish moss dripped from the trees, vegetation in every direction, aged logs laid across a forest floor covered in verdant moss, and a full spectrum of smaller creatures scurried about the earth. It was tranquil and extraordinary.

A gentle calmness overflowed me. To make things further sublime, Christopher was there with me. He even let me hug him.

A gecko sat motionless on a log, awaiting nothing. Christopher eased his hand in for a touch, but it scurried off at the last second. I smiled until he tried and failed miserably to catch it, only to fall over a log. Then I laughed. It seeped out. The spill he took left him with a mud-covered face when he rose from the muddy earth at his feet, and I lost it.

"Are you laughing at me?" asked Christopher.

"No." I snorted. "I'm laughing with you."

"But I'm not laughing."

"Okay, I'm definitely laughing at you then."

He squinted his eyes at me as I knelt beside him.

"You have to watch out, Christopher," I said. "There's snakes out here. Poisonous ones. Centipedes. All kinds'a creepies."

"That lizard's quick."

"The faster you move," I told him, "the faster it runs. Imagine if a giant were chasing you."

"I'm not going to hurt it."

"He—"

"Or she," he interrupted.

"—or she," I continued, "doesn't know that. We're just guests here. This place belongs to the lizards more than it does to us."

"Ohh, look. There's one!"

"Be still." I guided his head to three more lizards perched on a log. "They're everywhere. Just look around."

"I wanna catch one."

He dashed off to chase the gecko without another word.

"Dude," I said, "hold up."

I chased him, but he continued following the gecko into a lush green patch of bush.

"Stop," I shouted.

I rushed in after him but could not find him. Flora was thick. I pushed through it.

"Chris!" I continued calling. "Christopher, where are you?"

I came out on the other side of the shrubbery next to a lake. A layer of moss and algae-covered its surface only to be broken up as a sunbathing alligator scurried into the water.

"Christopher?"

"Over here, Dad. Come on. It's time to go."

Christopher was standing about half a football field

away to my right next to an airboat. A man was sitting motionless in the captain's chair. The large fan at the back of the boat chopped the air with threatening blades.

"Come here," I said.

"Come on, Dad," urged Christopher. "It's time to go."

I could not believe it when he hopped aboard that boat. I moved towards him and climbed aboard to stand beside my son as the enormous fans began to speed up. They increased the rush of noise and air around us until the boat left the shore.

"Dad..."

Christopher was no longer next to me. I panicked and whipped my head about in desperation. I thought he had fallen over.

"Christopher?"

"Dad..." he called.

He was standing back on the shoreline. It was impossible, yet there he was.

"Dad," he called again, "where are you going? Don't leave me."

"Stop the boat," I said. "Stop the boat."

I turned to focus on the boat's captain. It was General Shepherd, but he was motionless and ignoring me.

"Dad...come back." Christopher's voice faded as distance stretched between us. "Why are you leaving me?"

"Stop," I begged.

General Shepherd was smiling.

"Pleeeease," Christopher continued, "doooon't leeeeaaaave meeee."

26-3 RESULTS

I opened my eyes to see Anthony slumped over in the corner of the room, patting his belly. He was bloated but feeling okay so far.

"Still holding up?" asked Draven.

"Shit," answered Anthony. "My ass is gonna be ready to eat again by the time you guys get to it."

Kat had fallen asleep in Elias's arms. The two of them made a cute couple, though I was not sure they would ride that train again. The two of them did not act like lovers but were close. Their eyes connected as if they wanted to rekindle an old flame. I hear intense situations have that effect on people.

I sat there, wishing they had met before things took a turn for the worse between my brother and me. The tower had brought us into the same zip code for the first time in years, placed us in a cell together, and pressed us into a situation where we needed each other. I figured I might even thank General Shepherd for it before I kill him.

"Dig in, D," he continued. "Shit's good as hell."

"You don't feel anything?" asked Draven.

"I feel full. That's what I feel."

Draven moved to the table, and Haley followed. They grabbed little bits of everything as if they were at a Golden Corral Buffet. It was the first moment of safety any of us had since arriving at The Tower. They were basking in it. We all were.

Elias brushed Kat's hair gently. "Kat."

"What are we doing?" Her eyes opened while she snuggled him in. "Are we about to go again? Can't we just stay here?"

"Nowhere, no, and no. Come on." He stood and pulled her up. "Let's eat something."

"Are you sure? Is it safe?"

"And delicious," interjected Anthony. "Trust…"

Elias went mainly for meats and complex carbohydrates. Kat wanted fruits and vegetables but grabbed lobster before walking away. I had not made my way to the table yet.

"What's up with you, Archer?" asked Draven. "Gonna eat or not?"

"Maybe on the way out."

"Still waiting to see if anyone gets sick and dies?"

"Just want the energy I get from it to last as long as possible, but seeing if you get sick is a perk of waiting, isn't it?"

Draven shook his head and went back to eating.

"How you feelin, Big Man?" asked Anthony.

"I'm okay," I answered. "Why?"

"The veins and…you know. Just look a bit rough."

"Actually, feel better than I have in years."

"Well, you look like shit."

"That's what I hear."

A few snickered.

"You going to eat that?" Elias reached for Kat's Key Lime pie.

"Yes." She slapped his hand.

"Ouch. Lay off the dried tomato paste, girl."

"Tomato paste?"

Haley watched on as they bantered playfully for a few minutes. I could tell she liked Kat, but Kat did not swing that way. It was kind of saddening to see.

Kat was acting sweet with Elias, he was returning her smiles and batting eyes, and Haley was watching her intently the whole time, but they were oblivious to her or anyone else around them.

I felt for her.

"We're all almost done eating," said Draven. "You going to grab something or not, Archer?"

I stood up and moved to the table for Key Lime pie. It was calling to me. I loved that shit almost as much as mashed potatoes and bread. But I could not compel myself to grab any of them. The meat… I had to have it. Looking at it made the salivary glands in the back of my jaw salivate rapidly enough to cause cramps in my jaw. I grabbed one of four New York Strip steaks from a plate and tore them into my teeth. They were rare. Blood was still warm. A chemical romance made love in a mouth grinding with molars barely able to keep up.

Then I quickly ate another, finishing to see the others staring at me.

"You sure you're okay, Big Man?" asked Anthony.

I raised my hands to suck the juices from my fingers. They were a mess and the plate holding the steaks was empty. I had eaten all four in piranha fashion.

"You going to throw up now?" asked Elias. "Because you just ate like all of those steaks. It's like you were in a trance or something."

"You sure?" I asked.

"Yeah."

"It was pretty weird, Archer," said Kat, "like watching the National Geographic Channel when animals are eating something they just killed."

I could not explain it to them because I did not know-how. Elias was right, though. I was in a trance, zoned out on the blood and muscle tissue swirling my mouth as I ate.

"Let's go," I said.

"Now?" asked Anthony. "You don't wanna rest a minute after eating all that?"

I moved to the second door, cracked it, peeked out, and moved through it, knowing the others would follow.

CHAPTER 27

SWEAT

HUMIDITY WAS LOW in the corridor beyond our makeshift dining room's door. Its walls were dry and had powder over them from decaying concrete. The air zapped moisture from my throat like I had spent the day before chain-smoking.

"Is it just me," asked Haley, "or is it warmer in here?"

"Yeah," said Elias. "Draven's balls are about to start sweating."

"Already are, bro," said Draven. "Already are."

"Looks like a dead end ahead."

"There's something on the floor up there," I said.

An incline came upon us and felt to be nearly a 40-degree angle. Slow steps were needed. If we moved too fast, we would undoubtedly be sliding the other direction on our asses.

"Careful." My foot slipped a few inches. "Move slow."

"You don't have to tell me twi—" Kat slipped into a fast slide.

"Kat," shouted Elias.

Draven was pulling up the rear and grabbed her wrist as she went by. She had not slid enough to build up momentum, or else they would have both went down, not that there was anything to slam into at the bottom.

"Thanks." Kat steadied herself.

"No problem," said Draven. "Good thing you're light, unlike my boy's fat ass up there."

"I know you ain't talking about me down there, D," said Anthony. "This shit's pure muscle up here, baby. You hear—"

Anthony's feet slipped out from under him, and he headed down the decline on his back, taking out Elias, Kat, and Draven as he went. They slid to the end of the slope and partially out of sight. Haley and I were already laughing.

"Did you do that on purpose?" asked Draven.

Anthony answered through chuckles. "I… I…" He stood up.

He continued laughing, and the others joined in. I think we were all glad it happened. No one got hurt, and we needed a good laugh.

They made their way back up to Haley and me.

"Round two?" I asked.

"Round two," answered Draven, "but I'm in front of you this time, Anthony. For real."

We pressed on, awaiting another slip that would not be as funny as the first. They were breathing much heavier climbing the ramp a second time around and could not afford to waste energy. Not with unknown circumstances sure to be somewhere in our near future.

The top of the incline was only a few meters away. Our cores had to stay tight along the climb to keep stiff enough not to lose our grips, which Anthony and Kat had already proven. The suits we were wearing reflected the uphill battle with sweat-induced dampness as our bodies tried to cool themselves.

"Sweating to the oldies," breathed Elias.

"What?" asked Haley.

"She's too young for that shit," said Anthony.

"It was a—"

"Shhh," I interrupted.

We came to a point where it leveled out again after about a hundred yards. Everyone was breathing heavily. We waited for our hearts to slow before moving on.

"Everybody good?" I asked.

"Let's get it," answered Draven.

We moved down the new section of the corridor and found ourselves at a dead end. There was a circular maintenance hole cover in the ground nearly against the final wall. A stack of oven mitts rested on the bare concrete next to it.

"Looks like we know where to go next," said Anthony.

"Okay," said Elias. "But what are the oven mitts for?"

"Fuck outta me."

"Let's just get this moved." I grabbed the maintenance hole cover, reaching my fingers into a few of the sparse holes on its top. It was heavy. "Give me a hand."

Anthony reached in to help. We pulled it up enough to slide it to the side of the hole. It clattered loudly—slicing into our eardrums without mercy—when it dropped in the confiding area of the corridor.

Elias covered his ears. "Thanks for dropping that, guys. Appreciate it."

I investigated the hole. Heat rose from it like a freshly opened oven.

Anthony moved away from it. "God damn! It's hotter than an Angelina Jolie on Salma Hayek funk fest down there."

"It's warm," I said.

"Warm my ass. Let's give that shit a few minutes."

"Why?"

"You know, open an oven door to let the heat out. Besides, we ain't all jacked up on whatever the hell they drugged your ass with."

"At least we know what the oven mitts are for," said Haley.

"Agreed," I said.

We waited until enough heat exited the hole to have us sweating. We had to move, but where that hole led was not somewhere I was sure we could stay. Not for long.

I grabbed a pair of oven mitts and slid them over my hands. "Put them on."

"Are we really going down there?" asked Kat.

"Any other ideas? Want to go back up and get shot? We can always do that."

"Don't be a dick, Archer," said Elias.

Anthony and Draven stepped in and asked me to *be cool* and *check myself*. It took me a second to realize I was thinking about attacking one of them. But they were right. I needed to keep a handle on whatever was happening to me. I felt love for the group I had not upon my first arrival and needed to control new urges directed at those responsible for us being there.

"I'm sorry, Kat," I said. "I don't know. Something's… I feel off. Calm and peaceful at heart, but aggressive impulses are... I think it's getting worse."

"Is that why you snatched me off the cot in our cells the other day?" asked Elias.

"No," I answered. "That was because you're a dick."

I held my serious face for as long as I could before I could not hold back half a smile. Elias did the same, and the corridor grew privy to a gallery of laughter.

I gloved up, and the others followed suit, awaiting me to move into the hole, and I did. It was lit with a damp red hue and created a tunnel-vision effect across its length.

27-2 LADDER OF FIRE

Sweat beaded on our foreheads. An increasing temperature fought against the notion of heat rising as we descended. The ladder itself rose in temperature to match the hell we had been through that day.

"Is it just me," asked Elias, "or is this frickin' ladder getting hotter?"

"It's not just you," I answered. "Keep moving."

We descended further. The ladder continued to rise in temperature. My hands were warming fast in the mitts, and I wondered if we would make it to the bottom without someone falling. We needed to hurry.

"Speed it up, guys," I said.

"Good idea," said Kat, "because this thing's really starting to burn."

"Aw fuck," said Draven. "It's too hot."

The ladder's redness increased as it rose in temperature. My new friends were having a little trouble keeping their hands on it. They let go and grabbed at it again quickly with each rung to cool their palms. I was starting to feel it myself, and our shoes were smoking with burnt rubber scents filling the air.

"Dammit," said Elias. "Go. Go."

"I can't hold on," said Haley.

"Do what I do," I said. "Grab the ladder's edge.

Place your feet on the outside of it and slide down. Hurry."

I slid quickly down the ladder with the others following. Last down was Kat and Elias. They fell to the floor together, with Elias hitting the ground and Kat landing on top of him.

We were already shaking our gloves off and flapping our hands as they dropped to our feet, smoking. The shoes came off next. Kat stood and did the same. Elias was out of his before he left his back.

"Now it cools off," said Anthony with sarcastic inflection. "That's nice."

I looked to see the ladder cooling from light red to the cold tarnished metal before shooting skyward beyond reach.

"Ain't no goin' back now," said Anthony.

Kat leaned over and gave Elias a loud peck on the lips. "Thanks."

"Anytime," said Elias. "Wait, are you getting sweet on me again?"

"Maybe," she answered. "Only if you get me out of here alive."

Kat stepped away from him.

"Done." Elias stood with a cocky smile.

We waited long enough for the rubber on the bottoms of our shoes to harden; then, I moved to inspect a plaque on the wall. A number rested next to a door:

'8TH FLOOR'

No time was wasted. I moved through without hesitation, and the others followed as usual, but none of us had high hopes. The tower did not feel as if it were something anyone intended us to survive.

CHAPTER 28

MIRRORING MOVEMENTS

THE MIMICS ARE essentially Praying Mantis. They are not tall, necessarily, 6'0" or smaller. They are built for stealth. They wear dark, small, almost steampunk style goggles to protect their eyes from extreme light. They have superior night vision and are most dangerous in the dark. They are thin, shredded, and extremely fast when they attack. Their forearms are barbed like the insect.

They have mouths that can open MUCH broader than they appear that they would with rows of very sharp teeth. This is a moment that is unexpected when they try to bite the head off of one of the fighters.

We entered an empty room under 40-foot ceilings with sweat beading across our faces and dripping from our arms. The door slammed shut behind us and all but forced the others to do a 180. My eyes remained forward. I was captivated by the abstract and colossal space ahead.

There were two circular patterns on the floor generated by highly focused lighting from above. They were laser-like in their precision. It was interesting.

The circles of light were some 30 yards in diameter: one was on our side of the room, another rested at the opposite end, and a 10-foot gap of total blackness filled the floor between them. Everything else was equally dark and unnervingly quiet. I could not see anything but the lit circles. Nothing.

A door was visible in the distance but just barely. A key-card scanner was lit up next to it and highlighted by a single white light to draw our focus. We noticed something hanging high above the opposite circle of light as we neared the first. It was a key card, no doubt for the door on the opposite side of the room. It dangled by a lanyard too high for any of us to reach.

"I think we need that card," said Elias.

"Captain obvious," said Kat.

Elias snickered and shook his head as we came to a stop. "So, what now?"

"Maybe I can reach it," I answered.

"You ain't reachin that, big man," said Anthony. "Ain't nobody reachin that shit."

I eased towards the circle of light beneath the card, taking a few steps into the first circle as I went, but a fragile creature with steampunk goggles over its eyes appeared from the dark. It stepped into the second circle as I entered the first. I stopped. It stopped. I could hardly accept what was standing in front of me.

"The fuck is that?" asked Anthony.

I turned back to the group to make sure they were not following me. The creature was turning back to me with synced movements when I returned my line of sight to it.

"It's like a twisted funhouse mirror or some shit," continued Anthony.

"I think I'm freaking out here a little bit," said Kat.

I wiped the sweat from my face. So did the creature before me, but I did not feel as if it were mocking me. The movements it made looked intuitive.

It was like the other creatures in some ways—former humans manipulated for the sake of scientific progress—but a hell of a lot smaller. Its movements were smooth. Silky. It mimicked me with mirror image precision.

Its forearms were barbed like a praying mantis. Scars extended from the goggles on its eyes, reaching back to disappear into its earholes. I tilted my head and leaned in to examine as it continued to mimic my movements. Its deeply shredded, small, individual muscles caught varying levels of light as they rippled with its swaying.

If I held still, so would the thing in front of me, only it would start swaying a fraction of an inch or two after a few seconds passed. It vaguely reminded me of a video game my son played. Mortal Kombat, I think.

I took a step forward with my right foot. It took

one forward with its left. I paused. So did the creature. It swayed again when I stopped moving, like a praying mantis on the branch of a tree mimicking a leaf in a breeze. I moved. The creature mimicked. I stopped. So did it.

"Just kick its ass, Archer," said Elias, moving into the circle.

A second creature stepped into the opposing circle from the darkness to mirror Elias. I was unsure how many there could be waiting for us in the absence of light, but I did not want to find out. Not if I could help it.

"They're playing with us," I said. "Back up."

Elias backed slowly from the circle. The second creature copied him flawlessly until hidden in darkness.

"Stay there," I said. "We don't know how many of these things there are."

I and the mirroring creature approached our circles' centers.

"What are we waiting for?" asked Draven.

"Quiet," I said.

I exited my circle of light and entered the dark area between it and the other, but the frail creature held fast where it was standing. It was so skinny. I was not worried about it. I was a little nervous, but the damn thing looked like it would break like shattering glass beneath my knuckles if I hit it.

We came face to face when I entered its circle and paused once more to wipe sweat from my forehead. It mimicked me again. I wondered if, better yet, when it was going to attack.

The lighted circles in the room faded to black. All was dark for a moment. Time ticked. No one talked.

Walls around us illuminated a dim-blue hue. Something distressing came to light: a matching number of creatures in the distance—one for each human—were watching us. They slid their goggles up to their foreheads in unison. Strange muscles were where their eyes should have been. Distorted scars ran from their mouths to their ears. I was not waiting anymore.

"Fuck this." I launched a stiff jab.

It could see or sense or something. The creature slipped my jab and landed four of its own. It was a surprisingly embarrassing moment, but the creature had more speed than power. Blinding speed. I could feel my nose bleeding into my mouth, but I remained composed and moved in for a combination.

As we learned to call them, the Mimics slipped every shot I threw and fired back with shots landing high and low. It was an ethereal combination and severely off-balanced me. I would have thought such speed impossible had I not felt it myself.

It volleyed another combination. I covered as its barbed forearms sliced into my flesh and dropped me to a knee. The Mimic mimicked. I looked up from a knee; it looked up from a knee.

"He needs help," said Draven.

"He's got this," said Elias. "Give him a minute.

"Which fight are you watching?" asked Kat.

I surged from my knee as it threw another combination, but I took the shots and grabbed ahold of it, wrestling the wiry son-of-a-bitch to the ground and rained powerful blows upon it to bounce its head off the concrete. It did not take much for the frail creature to lose consciousness.

"That's one," shouted Elias. "You got this, Archer."

I hit it several more times until my fist pushed a few inches past the fragmented bones in its face. More for good measure. I kept hitting it until its face concaved an inch or so, then more. I do not know why. I just know I did. Venting… I must have been venting growing urges within.

"Archer," said Elias. "It's done, man."

I turned to see the group. The way they were looking at me… Their eyes said they did not know me anymore. Hell, I barely knew myself.

"Sorry." I stood. "I don't know what's going on inside of—"

My eyes grew wide when a second creature tackled me away from its fallen comrade. The speed of the impact made up for its weight and sent me rolling across the floor with surprising adrenalin. I did not stay down. My footing came back in cat-like fashion to face it.

"I'm going in." Draven rushed forward.

A third Mimic matched his movements and accelerated to spear him to the ground. It was pummeling Draven with a flurry of strikes of unrealistic speed. Elias and the rest of the group rushed in. So did the remaining Mimics.

A one-sided fight was unfolding around me. I did my best to match their speed while focusing on what the others were going through, but I could not. The agility of the Mimics was nearly impossible to counter. Inhumanly fast. Pinpoint accurate. Shots landed upon us like a mantis shrimp cracking a crab's shell for sustenance.

I circled my adversary to see Draven trying to stand, but a downpour of shots kept him down for a moment. He made it halfway up, and his attacker backed off when he fell again. Its mouth opened ear-to-ear to display a jaw filled with jagged teeth. An evil hiss followed.

"Oh Shit." Draven back-peddled.

The Mimic lunged as if it wanted to bite his head off. It might have done it too. Its mouth was open enough to fit his entire face in it.

Draven grabbed it by the throat to keep it at bay, barely holding it back. It repeatedly snapped like a rabid animal. Barbs on its forearms cut into Draven's flesh as he struggled to fend it off.

Kat stumbled backward into the one I was fighting after being hit and went right back to fighting the one kicking her ass. It looked her way as if to strike her in the back. I should have thanked her.

I attacked with a clawing strike while it looked at her, and its neck tilted violently. A second later and it dropped motionless at my feet. One more for the maker. I studied it and myself both externally and internally for a second:

claw marks on the dead Mimic's face were bleeding heavily, my nails were dripping with blood—thicker, longer than before. I felt a disturbing satisfaction.

"Help," called Draven. "A little help here?"

I moved behind the Mimic attacking him and broke its neck. That felt good too.

Draven eyed me. "Thanks."

I looked at Haley. She was being knocked to the ground repeatedly by a fourth Mimic as the others fought. Accumulative damage was stacking upon her. She needed help.

"Blindside them," I shouted. "Don't fight them straight up."

I spun to the other side of the one I was fighting, and it remained squared up with me, but at least I could see the others in the backdrop as we traded shots. Or should I say, while I tried to hit the quick bastard peppering me with combinations of fuck all if I know?

Draven slammed into it with his shoulder and knocked it off her. It was a heavy blow. The Mimic tumbled twice before springing back to its feet, but Draven kept charging in NFL fullback fashion to slam into the one Kat was fighting. It fell to the ground as well.

It gave Haley her first moment to take control of the situation. She was dizzy but attacking the downed enemy to beat it lifeless. She was tough like that, but I was unsure how much more damage she could take, and her ability to generate power on her punches and kicks was diminishing.

Anthony and Elias kicked the one I was fighting in the center of its back as I threw an elbow. The triple impact sent its head wheeling backward. It flipped to lie motionless on the floor at my feet. A few kicks to its head, and we knew it was not waking up.

I looked up to see Kat rushing the last one, but Anthony stepped in to hit it with a big right. He missed and lost his balance. The Mimic was too quick. It ducked a high kick Kat thought was going to land.

"Gotcha." Anthony grabbed it from behind and slammed it violently to the ground with a grunt before pounding it into oblivion.

It was over.

Haley tried to walk, but she could barely stand and buckled a bit. Kat moved in to help her up. She needed to avoid getting hit in the head again—something I did not think was doable in The Tower.

My attention went back to the vital card hanging over us again. I tried to grab it, but it was not within arm's reach, not even jumping.

"Archer," said Elias. "Archer..."

"We need that card," I said.

My throat felt odd. I sounded different when I responded. My voice was deepening in tone and becoming raspy.

I scanned the room for something that might be of assistance, but there was nothing in sight. Nothing useful.

"Aright," I said. "Everyone over here."

The group joined my position as I pointed to the key card and turned to Anthony. "Big man. On all fours. Right here."

Anthony looked me over before dropping to his hands and knees under the card.

"Draven. Elias," I continued. "You two get on top of Anthony and me. Kat, climb up and see if you can reach the card."

I kneeled on all fours next to Anthony. Draven and Elias did the same on top of me and Anthony's backs. Kat climbed us: a foot digging into the left side of my lower ribs, up to Elias, and on top of our makeshift pyramid.

"I still can't reach it," said Kat. "Hold on a sec."

We felt a subtle jarring as she jumped to reach it.

"I can't. It's too high." She paused. "Haley, see if you can reach it. Get on my back."

I could feel our pyramid shifting as Kat went to her hands and knees on top of Elias and Draven. Haley had moved in to climb up on Anthony's side but slipped off.

"One sec," she said.

I turned to see her. She was not doing well. Her eyes were a little glossed over, and she was wobbly. She needed a doctor, and I doubted Dr. Kepler would be willing to lend her a helping hand.

"Be careful, Haley," said Kat.

"I'm fine," Haley answered with a lie.

She climbed again and tilted off-balance before Kat grabbed her by the hand to keep her from falling. We shook as she stood on Kat's back and reached for the card but fell. Kat tried to catch her. It destabilized us to the point of collapsing our makeshift pyramid.

Haley fell right through us, but we all reached for her while we tumbled out of position. Luckily, she landed on Anthony and me instead of hitting the concrete.

"Are you okay?" asked Kat.

Haley held up the key card. "Look what I got before I fell."

I did not think she had grabbed it before we went down. We smiled. All of us. Including me.

"Good job," said Elias.

"Yeah," said Haley. "Now, let's go.'

"Damn..." I cut my little brother a glance with a smile. "I like her."

Elias grinned. "Too bad for you she's batting for the other team."

I snickered and stood to my feet with the others. It was time to move. None of us wanted to, but it beat going back up and getting shot down by General Shepherd and his goons.

We moved to the door, and Haley opened it. I paused before entering. It was a mental hiatus to prepare for more violence. I was sick of the place, but part of me was enjoying the bloodshed. I could have used a shot of Bulliet Rye Whiskey right about then.

CHAPTER 29

FANS

WE ENTERED A dimly lit corridor drenched in sweat, but a pair of back-to-back ventilation fans at the other end of it produced a rewarding breeze. They were large, loud, and nearly encompassed the broader side of the corridor in their entirety. I would have found the tone annoying if that current of air was not needed so badly.

We dropped against a wall to rest. I looked towards the fans, where the hall shifted smoothly from its rectangular shape into a large square to house the fans. No doubt we would have to turn back or squeeze by them. The other end of the corridor was a concrete dead-end of greyness.

The vacuum generated by a swift current of air racing over us and towards the fans tugged lightly on our bodies. It pulled the hair on those who had it. Draven and Elias put their hands on their heads to take deep breaths of its cooling nature. Anthony put his hands on his hips and slumped down the wall to rest.

Haley bent over and threw up.

Kat rushed over to help her. "You've got a concussion, baby. Come here." She led Haley to the double ventilation system and helped her rest against a wall. "Stay here for a minute and rest. Take deep breaths to cool off faster, but don't go to sleep."

Haley turned to face the fan with freely blowing hair and took deep breaths. Her eyes closed as Kat talked to her. They were hard to hear downwind from us and so close to the fans.

"Haley," said Kat, "I said don't go to sleep. Go to sleep with a concussion, and you might not wake up."

"I know," said Haley. "I'm just closing my eyes."

"Okay. I'm watching you." Kat sat across from her and unzipped the top of her uniform to catch a flow of cool air.

"Kat?" asked Haley.

"Yes?"

"You think you would have dated me if you weren't with Elias?"

Kat smiled. "Yes. Maybe. I would have at least tried it out for a night."

Haley snickered weakly. "You know I've never been with a man?"

"As in ever, in your entire life?"

"Gold star, baby."

"Maybe you should try it if we get out of here."

"No thanks." Haley shook her head. "Dicks look like soggy balloon animals."

"Really?" Elias sat beside Kat. "This is what women talk about?"

"Should have heard what we were talking about the night you didn't show up for our last date."

Elias leaned his head against the stone wall and looked up. "I don't even wanna know."

"I'm still sweating." Kat fanned her shirt. "I was burning up in there."

"Damn straight," said Anthony, "but this shit feels amazing."

I walked to the first fan on the other side of Haley and stared into it. There was a door beyond the blades—an alternative way out.

Something inside me was changing for the better. I realized it while letting the air cool my skin and thinking about Christopher—wondering if I would ever see him again. I also considered whether he would think I abandoned him if I never showed up; I thought about forgiving Elias for everything because I didn't want either of us to die with unpleasant emotions harbored towards each other. Mainly me to him.

It was not all peaches and cream, though. I also thought about how much I would love to kill General Shepherd and his fruit loop posse of wanna-be tough guys, the creatures we had faced, and whether or not

I was becoming one of them. Part of me knew I was becoming happy inside as a person and finding a new unity. I had established a new love for my brother and life itself while going through everything The Tower had thrown at us. Another part of me was scared I would eventually hurt the others with animal-like predatorial instincts.

I could only hope the newfound peace I had searched so long for to overpower whatever those running The Tower were changing about me. I was becoming a double-edged sword and had to focus the good and evil towards the right people. For the others' sake and myself, I could not let it break my born-again humanity.

I glanced over my shoulder. Haley was seated on the floor with her hair still blowing in a forgiving breeze. My head felt as if fireflies were buzzing around inside of it, faintly zapping the inner lining of my skull.

It made it challenging to study Haley's face and grade her concussive state. I squinted my eyes tightly for a second to suppress the sensation. I accepted it. My head had done that now and then since they injected me.

Just a few minutes to relax... I needed it like everyone else. A deep breath with closed eyes, a long exhale, and a slowing pulse no longer matching rhythm with chopping ventilation blades seduced nervousness.

CHAPTER 30
OUR FAULT

EVERYTHING WAS BLACK as pitch. My breathing felt heavy. I was panicked and unsure why as I reached my arms out in blindness, spinning about to feel for anything I could touch.

The ground beneath me felt solid like steel. Air was cold with a sweaty scent. I had smelt it before. It lingers in gyms after a hard grappling session with 20 people going at it on the mats. Only nobody was wrestling. I calmed my breathing to focus when a distant noise caught my attention.

I jumped.

It was too dark to see. I closed my eyes to focus and tilted an ear. A moment of silence passed that lingered longer in my mind than it did on a clock. I needed to move if I was going to find a light source to see.

I took slow steps to avoid tripping over the unseen as I made my way through the dark to find a hint of light. Then one appeared in the distance. It was faint and seemed to come from nothing, but it was there.

"Where the fuck am I," I whispered to no one, "and where the hell is that coming from?"

There had to be a source somewhere. Eternal darkness is not possible in the world we live in, not outside the boundaries of our hearts.

I continued my slow walk until that noise reverberated against my eardrums again. It was quick. Haunting. Somebody was struggling, and it sounded like more than two people were going at it: feet sliding, an occasional grunt, the voice of three adults—one female, two males—too quiet to make out, and what sounded like a child. It was Christopher.

"No," he shouted. "I don't want… Get off me. Go away."

"Christopher," I called into obscurity with a quickening pace. "Christopher, where are you? Can you hear me?"

"No," he called out. "Stay away. All of you."

Dim light with no point of origin slowly lit the world around me with an even hue of off-white. I was not outside. There were no trees, grass, or dirt ground beneath me, stars, suns, or a moon in the sky, and no sensation to reveal even a hint of airflow. Nor was I inside. There did not seem to be a roof over my head—or any walls for that matter. Nothing but an endless hard floor and open-air surrounded me. I could see them in the distance coming into view, but they were too far away to make out.

I ran.

The closer I got, the more into view they came, but the distance between us was not closing fast. Three adults dressed in black pants and matching long sleeves came into clear view. Their faces remained hooded behind black ski masks with only their eyes showing, and they were dragging Christopher away from me.

"Christopher," I shouted again.

"Stay away from me," he called back.

I was closing in on them and ready to inflict some severe damage when I got there. Christopher was kicking and screaming. Like me, the boy was a fighter at heart.

30-feet away. That is how close I was when they let my son go, and he turned to look at me. He didn't run. He just stood there in the middle of them, staring at me with his hands at his side—a blank expression. The three that had him were motionless as well.

"Christopher," I said. "Come to me."

He started walking backward with slow strides and an emotionless expression. Something was wrong with him.

"Christopher," I asked, "what are you doing?"

He kept backing up as if something terrifying was creeping up behind me. I spun a 180 to find nothing. When I turned back to him, his distance had doubled from me and the three standing between us.

"What the hell did you do to Christopher?" I walked their way.

Their right hands move to their stomachs, palm in, and opened with wide fingers in perfect harmony. I stopped, worried all three had a gun, but their hands moved upwards until they covered their faces, grabbed their mask, and pulled them slowly from their heads.

My breathing became erratic again when I saw them. It was Christy, Elias, and… And me.

My head shook involuntarily.

They took steps backward, matching Christopher's pace as he continued to distance himself with eyes locked on to me in the backdrop until he began disappearing into the darkness. Confusion would be an understatement. I was scared for the first time in years.

"This is my fault," said Christy.

"This is my fault," said Elias.

"This is my fault," said the other me in black.

Then they spoke in sync, "This is our fault. All of ours."

They disappeared into a darker region as I watched Christopher in the distance until he grew barely visible. He shook his head at me in disappointment, turned, and walked to disappear into nothingness. I was alone, and what little light there was faded black is pitch again.

"Archer," called Christy from nowhere.

"Archer," called Elias from nowhere.

CHAPTER 31

BEYOND THE BLADES

"ARCHER," CALLED ELIAS.

I woke. I cannot say another moment of peace was missed waking up from that dream. It was not a serene instant with my son but a nightmare communicating a message of truth. It signaled Christopher's anguish and the fact we pushed him away by not handling the situation better.

We should not have isolated ourselves. Instead, we should have stayed strong for him and gathered at birthday parties and such without fear of fighting. If I never found my way out of The Tower and back to Christopher, he'd most likely pull further from the light and recede into the darkness I once let envelop me.

"Christopher," I whispered to myself.

"Christopher's not here, man," said Elias. "We're starting to worry about you."

I looked around. The others were staring at me again. It took a second to gather myself.

"I'm okay," I said.

It was an untruth. The others knew it was, but what was I going to say? That I was beginning to have impulses that might be dangerous? It is not like I could separate from them, and I would be damned if I were about to tell the others I had an urge to take a bite from one of the Mimics.

"You don't look okay, Archer." Elias shook his head. "I'm used to you talking to…you know…your son and whoever, but something's happening to you. Look at your arms. Your hands and your eyes… They're…"

I ignored him. I ignored the subject. There was nothing anybody could do about whatever the hell was happening to me, and there was no need to dwell on it.

"You see that door?" I asked. "The one behind the fan? We have to get there."

The others stood as Elias and Kat approached Archer.

"Through there?" Haley eyed the spinning blades. "Seriously?"

"Dead serious," I said. "Unless you want to go back up and get shot."

The group was gathering in thought and listening to my every word. They were most likely hoping someone would come up with a better game plan, but we were not in the luxury of swimming in options.

"Okay." Elias took his attention from the spinning blades and directed it at me. "Fuck it. I'll go first."

He moved to the blades. They were loud, spinning fast, and thudding air with each pass. One wrong move would turn him into a fleshy liquid confetto.

He laid on his back against the bottom left corner of its metal frame to shimmy through a small gap, hoping not to get cut. His left shoulder was inches from spinning blades as he inched his way through the tunnel. It took him a bit, but I was not worried about him. He was lean and agile. Once he was clear, he stood in the 10-foot space separating each fan.

"Okay, Haley." He paused to think. "Someone needs to help Haley from that side. I'll help her from here." He motioned towards the second fan. "Next one's going to be tight."

I could not argue. There was a good amount of space between each fan for him to assist her, and Haley needed help, but there was less room to squeeze past the second set of blades than the first. They were less than an inch from cutting into the square passageway's top, bottom, left, and right sides.

Kat helped Haley through the space between the first set of blades and the wall. She was smaller, but it was still more dangerous for her than the others. I feared she would panic in her disoriented state or make an improper movement leading to injury or worse. Kat had to save her twice: Haley's knee would start to rise, Kat would pull her foot to straighten her legs again, and Elias would pull her through a little more by the hands. This repeated a few times, with the rest of us coaxing Haley to stay straight like a 2x4 and let the others do the work.

"Careful, Haley," said Kat.

Elias regripped Haley's hands. "Straighten your legs and don't move."

"Okay," said Haley.

He pulled her the rest of the way past the fan and helped her stand. "That's one. One more to go."

Elias shimmied beyond the second fan as we watched with nervous expressions. His passage beyond it was a tighter fit. If someone were going to get cut, it would be by the second fan, except for Anthony. He was a big guy. Even the first would be tough for him.

"All right, Haley." Elias stood beyond the last fan. "Don't try to come through this one on your own. It's tight. Just lay down and reach through like last time. Me and Kat'll slide you underneath it."

Haley laid on her back and reached her hands slowly past the blades. Elias grabbed them as he dropped to his ass and looked at Kat. "You ready?"

Kat nodded and locked eyes with Haley. "Keep your legs straight and don't move. Play dead for us here."

"Okay," said Haley.

Elias pulled a bit, inched his butt back, and pulled again, repeating the process until Haley was hip-way through the chopping blades. She lifted her knee and moaned.

"No, no, no, Haley." Kat pulled her feet to straighten her legs. "You can't do that, baby."

"My shoulder," said Haley.

"Just a little bit more," reassured Kat. "That's all we need from you here."

"Come on, Haley," shouted Anthony.

"Yeah," Draven joined him. "You got this."

Haley nodded as we continued our support. We were becoming more family than friends by the minute, and it felt good. I would even go so far as to say it made my heart warm the coldness brewing inside me.

Elias eyed Kat with dreadful eyes and pulled her again, concerned over the possibility of watching his friend get chopped into pieces. I felt what he must have been feeling. The blades were rotating downward where we had to pass through and no doubt would snatch her to its center if it caught her good enough.

"Here we go," said Elias. "One… Two… Three."

Haley winced as he pulled her a few more times. They cleared the second fan, and the others high-fived around me as she stood. It relieved stress to know she would be safe and a small victory we all needed.

Draven told Haley he knew she could do it. He was justifiably confident in her, but truth be told, I could tell she was worse off than she let on. The girl had too much pride to reveal her concussion-induced weaknesses.

"Hell yeah, girl," said Draven. "We'll be here for you all day, baby."

Draven moved in and calmly made it past the first

fan. He paused to think about the second fan and looked at his knuckle. There was a small cut. It was the least of worries in The Tower, especially with a tighter sealed fan next in line to conquer.

He made passing the second fan look more effortless than the first. Draven—a playboy at heart—often surprised me with his compassion towards treating women with respect and his abilities in the cage; passing through that second fan so swiftly was no different.

Draven stood and hugged Haley. "You good?"

"Yeah," she answered. "I'm fine."

I turned to Anthony. "You ready?"

"Why don't you go on ahead, big man?" answered Anthony.

"You do know you're nearly twice my size?"

"Still a bigger man than me."

"That's a new one, but I'll go after you. Just suck that heavyweight gut in."

He laughed, patted his belly, and did a curtsy before entering. But the comedy stopped when those blades grew close. It was too tight for him. He inhaled deeply, sucked in his gut, and inched his way through the first fan with us on edge.

I do not think any of us breathed until he made it through and stood. The others were most likely thinking the same thing I was—*the second would surely cut him.*

"Okay, Anthony," said Elias. "Get your big ass over here."

I dropped down and eased past the first fan as

Anthony approached the second set of blades. I stood once I made it, knowing he would not be able to make it beyond the second alive.

Anthony was bigger than he thought he was. He was one of those chubby heavyweights with body dysmorphia. There was no chance in hell he was squeezing past those blades.

He came close to them and stopped. "I won't fit."

"Putting on some weight, big homie?" Draven chuckled. "Just suck that shit in like Archer said."

"You guys press forward," I said through the chopping blades. "I'll circle back with Anthony, and we'll find another way."

"Fuck that." Elias looked around. "We ain't leaving you. Look for something solid. We gotta stop this thing."

They searched the immediate concrete encasement on the other side of the fans blocking Anthony's path. It was larger than I thought it would have been, but it was empty of all but a door. I was sure they were wasting their time, but I remained silent to avoid crushing hope.

"There ain't shit in here." Draven opened the door. "Maybe down the stairwell here?"

I could not see it, not the stairwell. I could only see those in the other room standing beyond the fans.

"No…" Kat walked to the door and eyed its metal frame. "Wait."

She kicked its frame over and over with hard, stomping push kicks—setting her hip into each—but it would not budge.

"Hey," Haley said with a weakened joking expression. "Didn't think a door frame in a compound like this was just going to give way, did you?"

Kat stepped back for one more solid kick out of desperation more than anything else.

"The rail," said Haley.

"What?" asked Kat.

"The handrails on the steps."

Elias and Draven eased towards the door.

"What you got?" asked Anthony.

"There's like a six-foot handrail just inside the door," said Elias. "Leads down a few steps before the stairwell cuts off somewhere else."

They moved into the doorway and beyond my line of sight, but I could hear them trying to force the handrail to surrender its grasp on the wall. Anthony and I waited until they came out breathing heavily some 10 minutes later.

"We got it loose," said Elias, "but can't get it to come off the wall."

"Try standing on it," I said. "All in the same spot."

"Want me to come stand on it for you?" asked Anthony.

Draven cut him a look and snickered with a shaking head.

I stepped to my left, moved dangerously close to the blades, and tried to get a better look. "How high are the ceilings in there? In the stairwell?"

"I don't know," answered Elias. "About eight or nine feet?"

"Is the rail anchored into the wall or barred into the floor?"

Elias eased over to look. "It's mounted on the wall."

"Okay," I said. "Try standing on the rail together, and push against the ceilings with your hands to add to your body weight. Get all your weight in the same spot."

Elias nodded. "Okay."

Draven, Kat, and Elias went back into the stairwell. A few moments later and we heard a crash. Metal clanked about the floor.

"Mother…" shouted Draven.

"You okay, D?" asked Anthony.

Draven emerged, rubbing his elbow. "Yeah, just busted my shit when it gave way. I'll be all right."

He walked back into the stairwell, and metal clanks accompanied the sound of busting concrete as the handrail gave way.

"Got it?" asked Anthony.

They emerged with the handrail. A few bolts still held chunks of concrete to it.

"Damn right we got it," said Draven.

"Sharp, Haley," said Elias. "Good thinking." He turned to face Anthony and me. "Stand back."

I stepped back as he raised the railing to ram the upper portion of the fan.

"Hold up," I said. "Maybe we should move to the other side of the first fan in case this thing comes apart."

"Man," said Anthony, "I don't think I could make it back through in time if that rail don't hold very long."

Elias and the others looked to me, awaiting a response. I nodded, and he jammed the railing into the spinning fan.

PANK.

The spinning fan knocked it away and onto the floor, barely missing Kat as she fell upon bare concrete to avoid it striking her in the chest.

"Ouch," said Elias. "Son-of-a…"

"You and Draven throw it in together like a javelin," I said. "Do it as fast as you can and get back."

They did as I instructed and tossed the steel railing into the spinning fan like a harpoon.

It got caught and spun towards the top of the fan and bounced around as everyone took to cover the best they could. Anthony and I ducked until it lodged itself between the blades, frame, and support beam holding the motor. An ear-piercing screech filled the room as it slowed to a grinding stop. The engine was still straining. Burning. Smoking.

The fan slipped and moved a few inches before coming to a halt again. Draven and Elias rushed in to hold it as Kat helped Haley to her feet. I guess she had ducked for cover as well.

Elias strained to hold the blades. "Hurry."

I moved through the blades with Anthony right behind me. Elias and Draven were straining to the point of exhaustion, trying to hold it still, but the unit was slipping. We needed to make haste.

Kat was bouncing in place. "Come on, come on, come on, come on, come on."

I made it through just as it started to slip and helped Draven and Elias hold it.

"Anthony," said Draven. "Hurry, bro."

It moved an inch or so before I grabbed a blade on the downward stroke side for better leverage. Kat moved to my side to help, but she could barely get a hand on it. We grunted as it started to give way.

Anthony was not entirely out when it slipped. The blades ramped up and lifted his foot to the left before flipping him into the air as he exited. I reached out for the ground to cup his head not a second before it would have hit the floor.

Pieces of metal banged apart as the fan came undone. The handrail was beating dents and cracks into its frame. We ducked for cover again, and Haley screamed as a piece shot out and buried itself into her thigh.

"Fuck." She clutched her leg. "Really?"

Kat pulled it out. It was small. She would be okay; that is, as long as she could survive things to come in an already weakened state.

"Everyone okay?" I asked.

"Sure," answered Haley. "Great."

Kat dropped the piece of metal she pulled from Haley's thigh to let it clatter on the concrete. "What the hell's this place got against you?"

Haley snickered. “Couldn’t tell ya.”

“Everybody ready to go?” I asked.

The group acknowledged. I headed for the door and turned back to Elias before entering. “Thanks.”

He nodded, and we forged into The Tower’s depths.

CHAPTER 32

MUDDY WATERS

WE ENTERED A long staircase. Dim lighting tracked the ceiling's edges, but it barely lit our surroundings. It was as dark as General Shepherd's heart, as black as mine once was, but something about surviving with Elias had brought light into me. I still wanted to kill the soldiers and those leading them, but hate was fading, and that peace I once searched shadowy corners for was upon me.

"Why does everything gotta be so damn dark?" asked Anthony.

"Keeps it interesting," answered Draven.

"I'd rather be bored."

A hazy-blue hue of light emanated from the base of the staircase as the sound of water running came to the fore. Unseen bats squeaked somewhere ahead of us.

"Water?" asked Kat.

"Sounds like it," answered Elias. "Bats too."

A plaque came into view when we reached the base of the stairs:

'5TH FLOOR'

"That killed three floors," said Elias. "We're almost there. Almost to ground level."

The others gathered before moving forward. They cut curious eyes back and forth over the sounds of running water and bats. I was a bit curious where it was coming from myself. It was an odd combination of noises for an indoor building. Then again, nothing was ordinary about The Tower.

Anthony ventured ahead of us towards the blue hue. He was brave and, though I questioned his judgment walking in alone, it was nice to see someone else taking point for a change. Each of us needed confidence.

The others and I followed him to an arched, 50-meter, cave-like passageway with10-foot ceilings. A piped sprinkler system sprayed the muddy ground with false rain. It felt nice, refreshing, and cooled my skin instantly upon contact.

We stopped to enjoy it for a few minutes before moving on. It was hard to walk away from after being in the blistering room with the Mimics. Plus, we all needed a bath.

What started as firm ground beneath our feet grew softer with every step. Anthony slipped at one point and barely caught himself, not that there was anything dangerous to land on or fall off. But it was slick, nonetheless.

Draven reached down and took a handful of earth. "It's mud."

"No shit," said Draven.

The blue hue brightened to tint wet ground as we proceeded. Makeshift rain fell harder with each step, and our feet began to sink. We were ankle-deep before we knew it.

"This mud's getting thicker," said Elias.

"Again," said Draven, "no shit."

"I'm just saying be careful. I'm sure it's here for a reason."

Anthony was still leading me and the other captives as we moved forward. The torrent of falling water increased in intensity as we continued. It eventually became a heavy downpour.

Anthony turned to walk backward while addressing the group. "Least it ain't so hot we feel like we bout to—"

He fell chest high into a soft area of mud and grasped for the edge, but it offered no support. The earth crumbled into wet goo in his hands. He was sinking quickly.

"Anthony…" said Draven.

We approached the edge as Draven reached for Anthony. He was sinking into thickly aggressive quicksand and helpless against its desire to consume. We had to move fast.

Grab my hand," shouted Draven.

Anthony tried to reach his hand but was sinking too rapidly and beyond reach.

I grabbed Draven wrist to wrist and turned to Elias. "Grab my wrist."

Elias grabbed my wrist in the same manner that I had Draven's.

"Everyone," I shouted. "Wrist to wrist."

Kat grabbed Elias. Haley locked up with Kat, though I was not sure how much help she would be. If nothing else, her extra weight would help the rest of us from getting pulled in if things went south.

"Move in, Draven," said Elias. "We got you."

"Fuck me," said Draven.

I took my focus off the strength of our chain and turned back to Anthony. My eyes flicked about the muddy pit to find him, but he had submerged completely. Draven—now linked to the others—entered the mud pit frantically searching for his friend.

"Anthony…" Draven shouted before taking a deep breath and submerging with the rest of us, holding fast as we lowered him in.

Water pounded at our backs. Large droplets peppered the muddy surface and splashed it back into our eyes. Mud on your pupils is not something that makes for good vision and feels like shit to boot. It was not helping the situation.

I blinked repeatedly and shook my head to clear my eyes. It helped but not much. I turned my head skyward to clean them out with untainted droplets falling from above; then, I squinted and held them nearly closed to keep the mud at bay.

"Hold firm," I shouted.

Draven's arm shook and jerked in my grasp as he searched for Anthony.

"He needs to go deeper," I said. "Move closer."

We snaked nearer to its edge. I dropped to my knees. Then my stomach. Draven was down there for a while, and I was starting to think we would have to pull him up before we lost them both.

I waited until I could no longer. "All right. Pull him up."

With all my strength, I pulled a single-arm against the weight of two men locked beneath the tension of a heavy trap. A few seconds later and Draven's hand came into view. I had to reposition.

"Hold up." I shifted to my knees.

We pulled. A long beat passed before Draven's head cleared a muddy surface, and he gasped for air.

"Anthony's got my wrist," said Draven.

We struggled to continue pulling Draven and Anthony from the pit, but its edge crumpled under my knees, and I fell partially into the hungry mud.

"Archer," said Elias.

I fought to get back on solid ground as the others leaned back in a tug-o-war against life and death. My body slid to firmer ground and allowed me to get my feet under me again.

"Come on," I said. "Let's get them up."

We tugged until Draven's hips cleared the surface before Anthony's hand came into view. They were locked wrist to wrist like the rest of us and holding tight. We almost had him out. Anthony's elbow was coming into view, but his hand went limp and slipped from Draven's grasp. The sudden release of tension sent us falling backward and launching Draven to land, sliding at our side.

We scrambled to get up, but Draven was already diving headfirst back into our environmental antagonist. I lunged for his ankles and grabbed them as his waist cleared its edge. The others piled onto me so I would not slide in with him.

Elias and Kat grabbed Draven's legs with me, but we could not pull yet. Draven was still trying to get a solid wrap around Anthony's waist. We would have been right back to square one if we pulled him out before he had a good grip.

"Got him," said Draven. "Pull. Pull. Pull."

We grunted. We slid. We pulled.

It took a moment to get Anthony and Draven cleared from its deadly embrace, but things were getting worse. Anthony's limp body… He was motionless as we drug him away from danger's edge and to a firmer patch of mud.

"Help him," said Draven.

Elias checked his vitals. "He's not breathing."

I got on my knees beside his neck and shoulders, positioned myself over him, locked my elbows tight, and started CPR without hesitation. The heart can beat for ten minutes after someone stops breathing. He was not gone yet, and I refused to let him be.

Two-inch compressions using my bodyweight were hammering into his chest to keep him alive. I counted aloud as trained to do. Thirty compressions later, I lifted the back of his neck, tilted its head up, and gave him two breaths of air from my lungs until his chest rose a few inches.

I repeated the process a few times.

It took two and a half cycles of this with the others calling out to him—and Draven nearly in tears—before he started coughing. I pulled him up with Draven's help and patted his back.

"You're good, bro," said Draven. "We got you. You're good."

"Don't go that way." Anthony pointed to the mud pit and filled his lungs a few times. "That's not a good way."

The others laughed, patted his back, hugged him, and cheered. Anthony was a good guy hidden behind rough edges. I was glad he made it. We did not need to lose another life for both moral and survival reasons.

I approached the mud-pitted edge, scanning for a way around it. Rainmaking pipes lining the ceiling were a path of least resistance. They looked solid. I decided to test them.

I jumped and grabbed ahold of a few. "Follow me."

My hands held fast while traversing the pipes like a kid on monkey bars. The others watched me cross until I reached the far side of the cave and dropped off. They were most likely waiting to see if the pipes would hold my weight or not. I would have done the same.

It also made sense that I went first: I was already The Tower's chemical guinea pig, the pipes were sketchy and wiggled with each new hand placement as I traversed them, and there was no way to tell how large the mud pit that swallowed Anthony was. Everything on the ground looked visually the same, and I could have dropped right into it. But I got lucky enough to clear it.

I turned back to the group on the far side of the mud-pits. The others were close behind. One by one, they crossed.

The water rinsed most of the mud from our bodies as we scaled across the pit. It was nice to be clean again. It was nicer to be on solid ground.

We continued across the large cave until another blue hue lit the once black end of the cave. Makeshift rain slowed to a trickle. We were almost out of it and could claim victory over another one of General Shepherd's bent games.

CHAPTER 33

DARK CANOPY

THE JUMPERS ARE taller and thinner, like a basketball player. Think Grasshopper. The legs are large and disproportioned from the upper part of the body. The legs are very muscular, and they stand at a constant bend as if they could leap at any moment. The upper torsos are long but still muscular. The large over-exaggerated eyeballs are black like the other advanced creatures. They have sharp teeth and small barbs on their arms and legs.

The rest of the group was tight on my six.

We entered an area visually grand enough to leave the hardest caught off-guard. Everyone stopped the moment it came into view. It was unreal and hard to believe it existed indoors and cut off from the light.

The room was massive. Three gutted-out levels in The

Tower made room for an extremely high ceiling. It was an incredible sight: an indoor forest full of tall, leafless, eldritch trees, a small pond, and bugs flying about with bats high above chasing them. Moist, soft green moss clung abundantly to tree limbs. It was an entire living ecosystem confined to one massive room.

A giant ring of what I think was fiberoptic UV lighting wrapped the ceiling in a perfect circle. It reached nearly wall to wall and was at least 5-foot in thickness. It must have been keeping the trees alive.

"Didn't see this coming," I said. "Stay tight. Move like pond water."

"Pond water?" asked Elias. "What the fuck is that?"

"Just move slowly. Move carefully. With fluidity."

"All right, Bruce Lee."

They stayed close to me in formation, just as they had learned to do over the last few levels. We might have been ants to the creatures and those running the experiment, but we could deliver a nasty sting together. There is always strength in numbers.

We made our way across the interior landscape. A loud thump vaguely vibrated the moist earth beneath our shoes. We stopped to listen.

"Okay," asked Haley, "what the fuck was that?"

Another loud thump accompanied by a sharper vibration and the sound of rustling leaves filled the indoor forest. Bats stopped flying, bugs grew quiet, and a branch creaked.

"Uhmmm…" said Kat. "Can we keep moving?"

We walked across the earth-covered floor through leaves and grass. A four-foot black snake with a white head slithered across the ground at our feet

Draven jumped when it slithered over his shoe. "This is some weird—"

"Shhh…" I said.

"What do you expect?" whispered Draven. "Damn snake touched my foot.'

"Don't be a pussy." Kat shook her head.

We watched as the snake continued its slither and hid under a partially unearthed rock.

Branches on one of the trees rattled, no idea which one. We turned towards the noise but saw nothing. A tense moment passed before I signaled the others to move again. Kat only took a few steps before something caught her peripheral attention.

"Wait..." she whispered sharply. "I saw something."

She froze. We all did. We trained our eyes to follow her finger as she pointed skyward to the treetops.

"Are you sure?" asked Elias.

"Something moved," she answered. "I know it did. I swear it did."

An unusual silhouette crawled along the branch. It was hard to make out through branches and blue UV lighting, backdropping it with fake rays of sunshine. But it was a long, thin, black, humanoid silhouette.

"She's right," said Elias. "Something's up there." His brows raised, and he wrinkled his forehead as his mouth opened in fear. "Move."

The rustling and creaking of branches intensified as Elias yelled a single word—*Run.*

We tore through the makeshift forest as back-to-back sounds echoed out behind us like broken chatters. They were communicating, but it was not a language. It was a series of dark-toned, chirpy reverberations.

Thud after thud timed itself between the sound of creaking branches. I looked back for a second while holding my sprint. They were jumping from the trees, landing hard, and springing back up into them in pursuit of me and the others.

We were halfway across the moss-covered ground approaching a tunnel on the far side, but another thud left Elias hitting the ground hard. His face and upper body dug into the dirt as he slid to a halt. Haley and I stopped.

A tall, lanky creature with thick legs disproportionate to its upper body was on him. Its legs were held in a constant bend as if it could leap at any moment. Its upper torso was long and slender yet still muscular. The exaggerated eyeballs were black as the other creatures, and its teeth were sharp to match tiny barbs on its arms and legs. It looked like a grasshopper had partially taken over a man's body.

We rushed back to help Elias, but the damn thing sprung back into the trees.

Haley stopped and dropped to a knee, clutching her head in pain. "I don't think I'm making it out of here."

"Come on." I helped her up. "Stay strong, Haley. Be that mean ass little bitch we both know you are."

Another one of the creatures we came to call *Jumpers* landed on Kat. They hit the ground hard. It grabbed her up in its long arms to leap into the trees with her, but Elias lunged forward and wrapped his arms around her legs. Its mighty vertical leap lifted Kat and Elias several feet into the air before all three fell to the ground.

Anthony picked up a sizable dead tree branch as it stood. "Come on, mothafuckas."

He struck the creature with a powerful Hank Arron-style blow and knocked it over Kat and Elias, only to have it stand and surge airborne again. He stepped over his downed friends to swing again as it rose but missed. It landed behind him.

Anthony turned to face it as I planted the bottom of my foot into the back of its knee. It spun to meet me, but I was ready for it. Though, it did not matter in the long run; because Anthony cracked the branch over its head and knocked it out. Several powerful blows followed to send speckles of blood splashing his face.

We gathered around to study the tall, lean creature's remains: overly long legs, abnormally thick tendons resembling that of a grasshopper: skin lightly striped, and muscle was attached to tendons at unusual points on its limbs.

"Come on," said Elias, helping Kat to her feet.

Haley watched from a knee. I moved to help, but she stood and eased away from the group.

"Think she's going to be all right?" asked Kat.

"No," I answered.

Haley was overwhelmed, not thinking clearly, and shaking with fear. I had seen it many times in this war-torn world—she was becoming disorientated from brain swelling.

"I'm losing my mind." Her eyes focused on nothing as she spoke. "I'm losing my mind."

"Haley," said Kat. "Calm down."

"I want to go home." Haley staggered for a second and tried to run towards the entrance.

"Haley," shouted Kat. "Stop."

Another Jumper dropped from the trees and landed on Haley's back as she fled. It collapsed her hard into a cluster of roots below.

"No," shouted Kat.

It still haunts me. That moment it landed on her and the ones that followed. Haley was screaming in agony. It looked at us through the blackest eyes I had ever seen, both in color and spirit. Then the fucking thing spoke, repeating the words we had just heard from Haley—*I want to go home.*

It grabbed her and leaped back into the branches above with her in its arms. We tried to move before it took off, but she was too far away. It happened too fast.

Elias held Kat back as she tried to run under the spot Haley had been stolen from, but a splat stopped her struggles when Haley fell back to the earth.

"No!" screamed Kat.

We ran to Haley's aid, all of us, but the creature landed on her, grinned, grabbed her up, and sprung back into the air with her again before we could reach her. I'll never forget her eyes begging for help.

Its voice echoed from the trees with a crackle. Eerie. Sinister. Mocking—*I'm losing my mind. I'm losing my mind.*

We looked into silhouetting tree branches to catch a graphic image that could not be unseen: the creature was holding Haley down nearly two stories up while a third played with her broken body. Haley was moaning in pain. A wickedness of eerie sounds leaked out as the creature playing with her broken limbs copied her moans.

Kat buried her face into Elias's neck.

"I'm sorry," said Elias. "I'm so sorry."

Three cracks, the sound of breaking bones, were shadowed only by Haley's final screams before the thing broke her neck and draped her limp body over a large branch. The group was silent. I did not want to run anymore. I was ready to fuck shit up.

"Move in formation," I said.

They stayed tight and moved with me toward the tunnel as a unit. They had to. The two Jumpers above us were moving lower into their branches. We observed them. A third leaped next to the second. They rubbed their heads and bodies around each other like a pair of snakes, reinventing Haley's moans to create a bone-chilling sonnet of misery.

Kat fought to break free from Elias. "You sick, fucking freak, sons a bitch."

Both the other monsters leaped from the trees and landed at either side of us. The first to hit the ground took a swipe at me before dropping and launching itself over me, but it missed and got a taste of my claws as it passed overhead. The sound it made when I cut into it was an evocative opera of its darkness.

It landed in front of Elias and howled in pain over the five deep gashes I left bleeding on its chest, and its guts were exposed.

"Come on, bitch," said Elias.

I moved to finish the lanky thing off when the other slammed into my back and tackled me to the dirt. My mouth filled with soil as we slid. I saw Elias running after it, but I am not sure what happened to him. I was too busy eating dirt. Elias was picking himself up from the ground by the time I saw him again.

It stood over me as I rolled to my back to get my bearings. I was in a bad tactical position. Luckily, I was not alone in the fight. I had friends and a brother I had reunited my love with, and they wasted no time jumping into the mix.

"Let's get gangster on this mutha," said Anthony.

Kat blind-sided it with a round kick to its face, and Anthony hit it low with a back kick in sync with her attack. Then Elias joined in. When clear shots were available, it was overwhelmed with kicks, punches, knees, elbows, and the occasional smack from Anthony's tree branch. It was tough and handled what they threw at it better than any man could. Kat tried to take it down, but it leaped to the other side of us to avoid being surrounded.

It was clear they were not stupid. The Jumpers were

smart. I knew it was going to be a fight for the rest of us to get out of there alive.

Damn thing kicked Draven instantaneously upon landing next to him. He flew some 20 yards past us. It was unbelievable. They had strong legs, dangerous ones that left Draven clutching his chest and unable to breathe on the moss and leaf-covered earth.

That new instinct… The new rage inside me… I growled and revealed my claws in warning for it to stay at bay, but it did not heed to it. The Jumper wanted to fight.

It crouched down and lunged forward too fast for me to move. Just as Draven had been, it knocked me some 20 plus yards past a few trees. It hurt my chest, and I could only guess how Elias felt when he got kicked.

The second creature crouched for another attack. It would have pounced me while I was down, but Elias smashed it in the knee with a solid sidekick that bent its leg back in the wrong direction. Kat did the same, forcing its other knee to buckle incorrectly. The beast dropped, wailing as Elias stood to help them beat the life from it.

Anthony snuck up behind the last when it landed near the others and delivered an entombing blow to its head with the fallen branch. A merciless beating ensued. Nobody stopped until the Jumpers dead without question.

We gathered ourselves when it was over, but it took a bit for Draven to catch a good breath of air. He was okay but no doubt had a broken rib or two.

"This is going to screw up my cardio," said Draven.

We looked high into the trees before leaving. Haley was still up there. It was our final goodbye without a way to reach her. Kat and Elias wiped their eyes as we turned our backs to the trees. They were close to her over the years. It was a devastating loss.

General Shepherd was no doubt watching on a monitor as our group emerged from the forest with all but one left alive. His creatures were a failure. I hoped it cost him billions.

Anthony, Draven, Elias, and Kat followed me into the cave at the forest floor's far side, and we entered. No one talked. It was an unspoken moment of silence deserved and well-earned for Haley.

We stopped at a far doorway in the back of the opposing cave before entering the next room. There was a camera above the door. I looked into it and waved a clawed hand—a personal *Go fuck yourself*—before I smashed out the camera.

CHAPTER 34

BEYOND THE CAVES

WE MADE OUR way through the door leading us from the forest into a corridor long and wide. A stark contrast of cold steel and hard concrete forming around us was both comforting and unsettling. We were entering the eye of the storm, and another one of those fleetingly peaceful moments before the war was upon us.

The hall we were in was a long one. It was as if it went from one corner of The Tower to another without breaks, doors, or other intersecting corridors. The walk was unsettlingly quiet. Haley remained on our minds.

"Hello, Archer," General Shepherd's voice echoed the P.A. system.

I looked for another surveillance camera. We had seen them throughout The Tower upon our descent, but I did not care if they were watching us or not. I no longer felt that way.

"Take out every camera you see within reach," I said. "Let's pull some of their eyes from their sockets and see how they like it."

The others acknowledged my request, and I smashed out the camera closest to me, then another. The rest of the group destroyed cameras throughout the long corridor, but I paused, remembering what it was like to have a family. Christopher and those trying to survive alongside me were all I needed to be happy, and it took The Tower for me to realize it.

I still had new impulses, but I was learning to control them. I had not hurt anyone yet, and I would not. Instinctual rage focused on my enemy. I refused to pretend it was anything less than a desire to hunt. I needed prey, and that prey would be any that tried to bring harm to my pride.

I could feel Elias eying me.

"What's up with you, big man?" asked Anthony. "I mean…" His mouth froze open with worry. "You got fucking claws. And you're shredded like you're running a cycle of Winstrol or something. You ain't gonna be freaking out on us or anything, are ya?"

"They did something to me," I answered. "Must've been in that lab. I feel great, physically anyways."

Draven clutched his ribs. "Good for you. Give me some of that, 'cause I feel like shit."

"Seriously, big man," Anthony continued, "you good?"

I felt cornered talking to him like an alpha-male lion challenged for pack leadership, but I did not tell him that. I had it under control. I just needed to remain centered.

"He's right, Archer," said Elias. "We're worried about you. It's like you're turning into one of those things."

"I am," I said, "but it's something different than what they did to the others. Some new drug that I'm their first guinea pig with."

"How could you know that?"

"I'm certain of it." I heard something as I answered—a click in the distance. I looked to see nothing and continued. "I remember bits and pieces of their conversations from the day they injected me with it in that lab."

"That supposed to make the rest of us feel better?" asked Elias.

"Yes," I answered. "They're not controlling me, and I'm not losing control. Feels like the change is slowing down. Like it's almost run its course. I think it's messing with my head a little, though."

"Well, it's kind of freaking everyone out a little. Me too, if I'm being honest. This shit ain't normal. You look like some mutant or something."

I looked at the claws protruding from my fingers. They were steadily growing thicker than before—harder.

"And your eyes, bro," said Anthony. "They're getting

worse. They look like a… You ever see a lion's eyes? That's what they fuckin' look like… Like lion eyes."

"I know," I said, "but it's just physical. Mentally, I think it's settling. Slowing down."

That is when it hit me.

"Elias," I said. "That's it. That's what's going on here. They're trying to create a weapon of man. If we can find the doctor that did this to me, maybe we can end this."

I stopped. Something in the distance had ensnared my attention: voices, movement, and echoes.

"Soldiers," I said.

"How do you know?" asked Elias.

"I know. I can hear them."

"I don't hear anything," said Kat.

"Trust me."

I started walking again. The others followed.

"Okay," asked Kat, "what do we do?"

"We turn ourselves in," I answered. "At least until we have the chance to do something about it. We can't go back. They'll be guns at both ends."

"What?" asked Anthony. "Hell nah."

"Yeah. We turn ourselves in, but not really. We need to get close enough to turn the tables on them."

"Archer's right," said Elias. "If we make it through the next few levels, they're just going to kill us or make us start over again."

The ending segment of the corridor was coming up. Our only options were to turn left at its dead end or turn back, which was certain death by gunfire. The voices barely whispered as we neared the corner, but it was our best option. Better to restart our journey than to be executed.

"I'm with Anthony," said Draven as we neared the corner. "Hell no. I am not about to take myself over there and—"

"Too late," I interrupted. "Put your hands up."

Lieutenant Brice and his unit stepped around an upcoming corner several paces ahead of us. Weapons were at the ready. We stopped as soon as we saw them.

"Hold your fire," I said with a further altering voice.

"Get down on your knees," commanded Lieutenant Brice. "Now."

As he said, we did not have a choice, but it was all part of the plan. Two soldiers patted us down thoroughly, searching for possible threats we could have concealed as improvised weapons.

"They're clean, sir," said the soldiers.

"Thought the whole point of this was to see if we'd make it out," said Elias. "Now you're stopping us?"

"We're not stopping you," answered Lieutenant Brice. "We're relocating you to the next section of The Tower." He grabbed the com device on his collar. "We've apprehended the targets, General. Awaiting further orders to relocate for phase two."

"Good job, Lieutenant," said General Shepherd over the com. "Take the lot of them to the cages."

"Copy that, sir."

Lieutenant Brice turned back to us with a shit-eating grin. "Back on your feet. And boy, do I have a treat in store for you or what?"

We rose with the soldiers banging us around a bit. I did not like it. So, I attacked Lieutenant Brice as I rose, disarmed him, and gained control of the pistol at his waist. I had almost forgotten how nice it felt to hold a cold-steel barrel against an enemy's head. I should have thanked him for reminding me when I pressed it to his temple.

"Do you?" I asked. "Because I have a surprise for you. Tell your men to drop their weapons."

The soldiers aimed at me.

"You've got three seconds," I continued. "Two… One…"

Part of me did not care if they fired or not. A more vital part of me wanted to get back to my son. The lion in me wanted to kill.

"Wait," said Lieutenant Brice. "Wait. Do what he says."

His goons dropped their weapons quickly upon his command. Elias, Kat, Draven, and Anthony picked up the discarded weapons and pointed them back at the soldiers—a favor returned.

"Cuff the soldiers," I said.

Anthony and Draven cuffed the soldiers while Kat and Elias watched.

"What about him?" Draven motioned. "What about Brice?"

"He's coming with us." I turned to face Lieutenant Brice. "Where can I find the doctor?"

"A doctor?" he asked.

"Don't play games. The doctor. The one doing all this shit."

"Ahh. You mean Kepler." He pointed behind us down the corridor. "He's that way."

"Smart choice," I said. "Now move."

Brice led us through The Tower until we arrived at a door with a retinal scanner mounted at its right.

"Open it," I said.

"Lieutenant Brice," said Captain Warwick over coms. "What's your position?"

I gave him a golden, lion-eyed 1,000-yard stare. "Respond, and I'll stop your heart for you."

Lieutenant Brice looked at me for a moment before leaning into the retinal scanner and opening the door. He did not want to but held no reservations that I would kill him and take his eyes to do it myself if need be. No one, not even a man in Lieutenant Brice's position, wants their eyes clawed from their head.

34-2
DEFCON

We entered a high-tech section of the outer tower. It was abstract from the rest of what we had seen. The long, stainless-steel corridor was lined with doors every 20 or so feet. Everything was polished to a severe shine. Clear piping ran the ceiling with green, blue, yellow, and red liquids coursing through some of them. Bubbling black fluids coursed in a few others.

An ensemble of wires in various sizes and colors outlined the upper corners of rooms in the area. They were visible beyond the horizontal windows next to each door, and scientists were focused on work doing fuck if I know. The second window we passed revealed a series of jarred organs and someone pounding a keyboard in front of a monitor.

"Lieutenant Brice," Captain Warwick continued. "What's your twenty? Over."

I pushed Lieutenant Brice forward. "Keep moving."

Elias and the others raised their weapons to be a little more convincing. It did not take him long to decide.

"Captain Warwick," General Shepherd's voice echoed from Brice's walkie again. "Where are they?"

"Lieutenant Brice isn't responding, sir," answered Captain Warwick. "We're trying to locate him now."

"I'm going to need you to secure an escort team to take our guests to the helicopter," replied General Shepherd. "Checking cams now."

"Copy that. We'll—"

A piercing alarm wailed into my ears and echoed The Tower as walls around us flashed red from light sources of unknown origins.

"All units to tactical lockdown," said General Shepherd. "All units to tactical lockdown."

Several men and women replied over the intercom with confirmation. You did not have to be a genius to know something terrible was happening. Panicked voices, alarms, and red-toned flashing walls were a dead telling.

All visible personnel in the labs around us evacuated swiftly and rushed through the corridors. One by one, they ducked from sight when they saw us leading their soldiers at gunpoint, but it did not stop them from fleeing. Their only concern was getting to safety.

Alarms were not blaring without reason.

It was not because of us. Something more serious was happening, and I wanted to find the doctor responsible for my changes. I had to do it before we fled.

"Where is it?" I asked.

"Just ahead," answered Lieutenant Brice. "It is the second office to the left."

We moved forward unknowingly about to tumble treacherous dominos.

CHAPTER 35

DISCOVERY

WE ENTERED AN office with Lieutenant Brice in tow. Another door at the far end of the room had his attention. He pointed.

"That's his office." Lieutenant Brice took a breath and exhaled his betrayal. "His lab is just beyond it."

I shoved Lieutenant Brice to Elias. "Cover him. Everyone else, watch the doors."

A video camera on a tripod stood in front of a desk. He must have been recording something. If so, we had to see it.

It did not feel secure, but I placed the pistol in the back of my uniform without a holster with no choice otherwise. I rifled through the desk for a few seconds before noticing another security camera in the upper corner of his office.

"Are there cameras in every room of the compound?" I asked.

Lieutenant Brice did not answer.

"Answer, or I'll shoot you with your own pistol."

"Yes. Yes, there are, but only critical meetings, subject tests, and certain things are recorded for record. Everything else is on a twenty-four-hour loop."

"Subject test?" I asked. "You mean like the gauntlet you've been putting us through? Like what's happening to me?"

"Yes. Things like that and other forms of progress are recorded for funders."

"I want access to all critical meetings, and I want it now."

"I'm not—"

The pop was loud when I shot him in the foot. He screamed as he dropped. It was just the pinky. No doubt he would be in pain, but I needed him mobile.

"Access it now," I said, "or the next one's going in your gut."

He moved into position and accessed the computer's video files.

"Now," I continued, "pull up the most recent video logs on General Shepherd's meetings. All of them since they abducted us."

He sighed, but he did it.

35-2
SHEPHERD'S SUPERIORS

General Shepherd was in a meeting with several government officials seated at a long pearl table. They were in an enormous room with pearl walls. Sleek and slim monitors sat before each of them with a soldier in every corner. The men at the table were well-seated government hierarchies. I recognized most of them, but General Shepherd was swimming with sharks.

Secretaries of each U.S. Military branch were seated at either side of a table. Leading them was Richard Waterman, The Secretary of Defense, and Ms. Lynn Hollaway, the Deputy Secretary of Defense. General Robert Linderman, Joint Chief of Staff, was sitting at the head of the table.

"I knew half these people," I said to Elias, watching in disbelief.

"From serving?" he asked.

"Yeah. Not personally, of course, but my unit had several briefings with them over the years. Some under the radar."

I turned back to the feed.

Various others were taking notes along the wall behind the leaders in the video as they talked.

"Where's General Shepherd?" asked Holloway.

"Fashionably late, I presume," said Linderman.

The door swung open, and General Shepherd entered the room, immediately taking the empty seat opposite General Linderman.

"Sorry for the delay," said General Shepherd. "Traffic."

"Evening, General Shepherd," said Linderman.

"Good evening. Good evening to you all. I know why I'm here, but I want to assure you that things are progressing nicely."

"I appreciate that, but at this moment, we're considering termination of Project Blade. This conversation will determine what happens next. That is why you are here."

"As stated," General Shepherd paused. "I know why I'm here. And with all due respect, sir, that would be a prodigious mistake. We've made ground-breaking progress with—"

"General," interrupted Holloway.

General Shepherd was displeased with her interruption but remained cordial. "Ms. Holloway…"

"You've made some interesting progress," she said, "but it's taken far too long, and at a very high cost, to present us with a subject stable enough for field combat. We're considering other options."

"Other options?" asked General Shepherd. "We just need a little more time. We're not breeding kittens here."

"Time is the one thing that you're running out of, General. We've continued to fund and support your operation for nearly eight years now at substantial cost to the taxpayers. There are those high up who are uncomfortable with your progress, for lack of a better word. You have yet to produce a single field-worthy advanced soldier, General."

General Shepherd shook his head. "No. That is not right, Ms. Holloway."

"It isn't?"

"We're simply perfecting before a presentation. Listen, we're seven versions in on this thing. Moments away from LS8 and going to implement it soon. To stop now would be a monumental fuck up. Need I remind you that what we're doing here could save the lives of thousands of our soldiers and potentially millions of American citizens."

General Linderman was already shaking his head. "We understand the greater good and whatnot. The point is if you can't give me something to bring to the commander and chief that will knock his socks off, and I mean now, then I'm afraid it's time to shut it down."

An uncomfortable silence filled the air. It was nice to watch General Shepherd squirm for a change.

"I'll tell you what," said Shepherd. "What if I could put together a little something for you? Something that will, in fact, knock your socks off."

"What do you have in mind?" asked Waterman.

"A demonstration. I'll show you exactly what you're paying for."

"I'd hate to see it all go to waste," said Holloway. "I vote to give the General his opportunity."

"I'd be interested in that as well, Mr. Chairman," said Waterman.

General Linderman thought for a minute. "Fine. A demonstration then."

"So, it's settled." General Shepherd stood from his chair, gave a half-assed salute, and turned to leave the room. "Now, if you'll excuse me, I'm going to find a suitable subject for LS-8."

"Well shit," said Elias, "at least we know why we're here."

"Pull up this Dr. Kepler guy," I said.

Lieutenant Brice shook his head as he searched the video files. I watched him closely, waiting for him to try something funny so I could smack him upside the head with his pistol. It was not long before another video feed came onto the monitor.

CHAPTER 36

GOGGLES

A LARGE, CIRCULAR ROOM with a hollow core framed by cages against the walls on multiple levels filled the screen. A female scientist with a digital clipboard and a long white lab coat walked alongside rows of barred enclosures on the second level. She was taking notes. Something caught her attention on the floor next to one of the cages, and she stopped. We could not make it out until she picked it up. They were goggles, the same kind the Mimics were wearing.

She moved closer to the cage to peer cautiously inside. It was too dark for her to study whatever was in it. She moved towards the bars without worry.

Dr. Kepler stepped into view. "Back away. Do it very slowly."

The female scientist looked his way, trustfully worried, as she stepped back.

"What do you have there?" asked Dr. Kepler.

"A pair of Mimic light shields. They were just laying here."

Kepler extended his hand, and she handed him the goggles.

"Nothing happens by accident with them," said Dr. Kepler. "They're cunning. That is their danger. Open 115."

She entered a code into the digital clipboard and the door unlocked before sliding open on its track. She backed further away as Dr. Kepler approached the cage with the goggles in hand.

"Who's are these?" asked Dr. Kepler.

Rustling sounds echoed from the dim room behind the 115 cell bars.

"I'm waiting."

The upper torso of a strange creature leaned into the light. Its eyes squinted behind its abnormal muscular tissue. It moved cautiously.

Dr. Kepler handed the goggles into the darkness for the once-man creature to grab. "Gideon, keep these on, please."

The Mimic yanked him into the cage as the female scientist screamed.

"Jesus." Draven covered his mouth, watching.

"The fuck?" asked Anthony.

"Quiet," I said.

The female scientist ran to her right, paused, then to her left—panicking and not thinking clearly.

"Stop," shouted Dr. Kepler. "Now. I said stop this."

The female scientist looked from left to right before rushing to a com button on the wall and driving the palm of her hand into it. "Security to lab five. Code black."

A few impacts echoed from the dark as it tossed Dr. Kepler about. He came back into sight when they slammed him against the bars in view of the security camera. Multiple Mimics were attacking him, three of them that I could see.

"I said stop it." Dr. Kepler struggled for a moment and shouted. "Goliath…"

That is when this massive thing stepped into the frame: heavily muscled, thick skin with rhino-like texture, small eyes, and a weight I could not have guessed. It was hard to make out minor details, but it was far from pretty.

Its voice was deep, scary. Goliath, as he called him, stopped the attack with a single word—*Enough.*

The trio attacking Dr. Kepler retreated into the 115 cage as he crawled out and stood to his feet.

"Go..." continued Goliath. "Now, Dr. Kepler."

Dr. Kepler wasted no time surfacing from the shadows of 115. His white lab coat was torn and tattered.

A slice of it near his upper right shoulder ran wet with blood. The cage slid shut just after he exited.

Four soldiers rushed in and grabbed Dr. Kepler to help him, but he was pissed.

"Don't touch me." He shoved the soldiers away.

Dr. Kepler investigated the cage. "This will have consequences, Gideon. All of you." He turned to the leading soldier. "Terminate them. Do it where the others can see." He turned to push through the soldiers, punching in a code on a transparent panel before he exited.

The cell lit up blue with shocking electrical currents moving from the back of the cell to get brighter as they neared the front, forcing the mimics out. The door closed behind Dr. Kepler as the soldiers raised their rifles and opened fire, leaving the female scientist to cover her ears as the Mimics fell.

The video ended and left us wanting to know more. I would get Lieutenant Brice to show us another, whether he liked it or not. At that moment, he was without options and had to follow my orders to keep the air in his lungs.

CHAPTER 37

GEORGE

BRICE CLAIMED THERE to be only one viewable file regarding Project Blade. I did not believe him. He was either going to show me something else or take that bullet to the gut I promised him. His head whipped to the side and matched Dr. Kepler's shoulder in color when I smacked him in the temple with the pistol.

"Archer..." said Kat.

I cut her with a quieting look and turned my attention back to Lieutenant Brice. "Anything else?"

He was dazed but picked himself up from the floor. "Okay. There's one more."

Lieutenant Brice pulled up a row of video files for us to see, then clicked the first and a file loaded onto the screen.

A date code popped up before playing the video:

'V-LOG #1 - DATE CODE: 746BC89-0'

A vibrant and healthy Dr. Kepler was speaking from the lush seat of a private jet.

He was thrilled and energetic about something.

"I'm excited to meet Beijing's top Molecular Biologist," said Dr. Kepler. "What he's suggesting is revolutionary. I'm talking about the first attempt to interrogate the genetic basis of human brain origin using a transgenic monkey model here. They're hoping my LS virus will escalate their results."

Dr. Kepler panned his camera across the aircraft until a straight-faced Captain Warwick was in the background. The video ended.

A new one started:

'V-LOG #2 - Date code: 863BC90-1'

He smiled youthfully when the video began. "Here we are. Meet Dr. Han Suyin, the woman who cracked the code."

Dr. Han Suyin looked over her shoulder and smiled. "Ni hao."

"You'll never believe what they've done," continued Dr. Kepler. "They've inserted copies of the human MCPH1 gene, crucial for brain development, into ten primates. Five died, but five showed strides in cognitive functions. What we're hoping to do is bond my Larcos Supios serum, LS-1 for short, to the MCPH1 gene and multiply success to an untold degree. LS-1 attaches itself to nerve endings, the muscular-skeletal system, and macromolecules in the human body for rapid reconnection of torn cellular tissue; this expedites the healing process of things ranging from broken bones to surgical incisions and, under the right conditions, even traumatized brain tissue. The speed of its effect is pure nitro."

Dr. Han Suyin approached him from behind. "Are you ready, Dr. Kepler?"

"Born ready." Dr. Kepler turned back to the camera. "Signing off. Wish us luck."

Kat and my little brother looked anxious to get moving. They were all but pacing in place. Fidgety is a fair way to describe it.

"Archer..." said Elias.

I held up a finger to silence him. I wanted to know what was happening to me.

"Listen," said Lieutenant Brice. "You know Shepherd's gonna fry your ass when he catches you."

Elias bumped Brice in the back of his already bleeding head. "Shut the fuck up."

"Shhh…" I said as the following video started.

'V-LOG #3 - Date code: 871BC91-2'

Dr. Kepler adjusted the camera. "George seems stable. In good spirits even. LS-1 has outperformed all expectations. Take a look."

Dr. Kepler turned the camera to reveal a chimpanzee

and held three fingers into the frame. "George. How many fingers?"

George wrote on a small chalkboard and turned it to Dr. Kepler. A number was written on it—*3*.

"That's all I have for the day," said Dr. Kepler. "It might not seem like much, but this is only thirty-four hours after the LS-1 variant was added with Dr. Han Suyin's techniques and applied to George here. Stay tuned."

He turned off the camera.

He must have piqued the rest of the group's interest. They stopped fidgeting to watch.

"What is this?" asked Kat.

"An origin story," I said.

Another video log loaded.

'V-LOG #4 - Date code: 882BC92-1'

George was taking various cognitive assessment tests as Dr. Kepler talked and fiddled with a Rubik's Cube. His focus was on the camera, not on George. Draven snickered when George unzipped and rustled through the doctor's backpack behind his back.

"George is doing remarkable," said Dr. Kepler. "He's surpassed all the other so-called smart apes we've seen in the past. At this point, we're hoping he's—"

George hopped into his lap with an open jar of peanut butter, fishing the last of it out with his fingers.

"Didn't I tell you to stay out of my things?" Dr.

Kepler set the Rubik's Cube on the desk and moved to grab the jar from George. "You're going to get me into trouble."

George swatted his hand away and hopped onto the table aggressively.

"Well, I guess someone's having a bad day." Dr. Kepler grabbed the camera and moved to angle it on George's work, presenting a basic Lego construction and simple math.

"Check this out," he continued. "This may seem like a small thing, but he could not differentiate mathematical characters just a few weeks back. In this time, he's not only learned to read the basics of the language but to decipher it."

He moved back to the desk. Pausing. Shocked. Speechless.

"Oh my God." He turned the camera to George. He was holding the Rubik's cube, and it was solved. "Dr. Suyin…" he called and turned off the camera.

'V-LOG 5 - DATE CODE: 910BC25-3'

Dr. Kepler was walking through what looked like a primate facility lab when the video restarted.

"The genetic difference in DNA between apes and the rest of what we call humanity is roughly only 1.2%," said Dr. Kepler. "That 1.2% is the difference between peeling a banana and composing a symphony, building the skyscraper, or putting a man on the moon. Now, imagine my brain times of a fold magnitude greater by three or more. That very notion's why I proposed human trials to the Pentagon last week. They've denied me. They just don't get it. LS is ready, and I'm about to prove it… on myself."

'V-LOG #5 - Date code: 910BC25-3'

Dr. Kepler was slow to start talking when the video feed returned. He was deliberate in word choices, but something was different. George was in the background sitting in the corner of his cage with a depressed posture.

"George hurt one of the doctors pretty badly today," said Dr. Kepler. "They're pretty upset about it." He paused to scratch the back of his neck or feel for something before walking over to George's cage. "George is also losing patches of hair. So am I. And I'm not exactly sure what the factor is yet."

Dr. Kepler put his palm against George's cage. Feint black veins like the ones running through my neck, face, and arms were visible near then base of his skull. They had not been there in the other video logs. Not in the ones I had seen.

George looked at the doctor for a moment. They shared a moment of eye contact before George placed his palm against Dr. Kepler's, who forced a smile before ending the video.

'V-LOG #6 - Date code: 925BC31-1'

Dr. Kepler was pale by the time he uploaded the next video. Veins we had seen earlier on the back of his hand were webbing forward from his hairline to his forehead, his hair was thinning badly, and he lacked expression. It was fucking weird. He never spoke. He just stared into the camera for a minute and ended it.

That was the last video.

"Not quite what you expected, was it?" asked Lieutenant Brice.

I palmed the back of his neck and wrapped my still growing claws around it, resting them upon his carotid artery.

"We're leaving," I said.

"Yeah," said Draven. "I've seen enough of this freakshow."

"Agreed," said Anthony. "Let's get the fuck out of this place."

I guided Brice towards the other door.

CHAPTER 38

KEPLER

WE SOON FOUND ourselves in a laboratory with rows of large cylinders filled with failed experiments.

"Disgusting," said Kat.

She was right. It was gross—tall cylinders filled with yellow liquid housed partial mutations. Blue gobs of goo moved from bottom to top and backed down again like a sinister lava lamp enclosing improper metamorphoses. Not even General Shepherd would do something like that to a baby.

"Playing god…" I said.

"What?" asked Elias.

"These things are young." I looked around. "Looks like they're trying to grow them in a lab."

"Test tube babies," said Kat.

"More like test tube monsters," said Draven.

"I don't give a shit what it is," said Anthony. "I want my black ass out of this damn place. That's all I got to say."

"Agreed." I continued looking over the little creatures.

Whatever liquid they were in was preserving them. They could have been fresh or sitting in those jars for a decade. There was no way to tell. Either way, dozens of them lined the tables representing one genetically altered failure after another—shit for the can.

I stopped to assess one of them when something caught my attention. It was the creature's nails. They were like mine, only smaller.

Kat pushed ahead of me and stopped to look closely at one of the other bodies. I glanced to see what she was eyeing. A USMC tattoo was on its shriveled shoulder, and its face was disfigured, contorted into abstract art through biological manipulation. Then I looked at what used to be my nails again.

Kat screamed and jumped back. The group's heads whipped her way, and they rushed to her side.

"You okay," asked Elias. "What happened?"

"They're alive," answered Kat.

The muscles in its freaky head twitched. The head moved.

"Let's keep going," I said.

A man stepped from the shadows beyond some of the filled tubes down the way. The group raised their firearms, and he halted. I recognized him. The man from the lab was the same in the video logs we had just watched.

"Kepler..." I said.

"Dr. Kepler," he said. "Yes. I am he."

Brice reached for the pistol in the back of my uniform. He did not quite make it. I saw it coming in what felt to be slow motion and reacted without thinking, severing his carotid artery before he could reach it. I could feel my nails parting muscle as they swept through tendons, but I never took my eyes off Dr. Kepler as he fell to the floor.

Dr. Kepler was the only one besides me that did not flinch. The others stepped back while Lieutenant Brice flopped around a bit, clutching his throat. Then he was still.

"Spectacular," said Dr. Kepler.

"Your turn." I opened my bloody hand hip-level.

"Hardly." He paused and looked at me for a moment with admiration in his eyes. "Mountains have been climbed, but what I have created still proves unstable. I confess, I was beginning to think that it could not be done. Then you came along, the sole subject of LS-8. You have maintained the cerebral acumen of your humanity. I would dare to say I improved and adopted only the needed attributes of your animal gene. You are my greatest success."

"I didn't ask for this," I said.

"No, you did not, but you did not thank me either."

"What you're doing…" said Kat. "This has to stop."

"Agreed," I said. "How many lives have you sacrificed?"

"As many as were needed," Dr. Kepler moved a small desk to rest his hand on it, "but none of these conversations matter. In fact, none of this is of matter anymore. This place, like your body once was, is nothing more than a prison for all of us."

"Then let's burn it down."

Dr. Kepler smiled. "Something we agree on."

"I want you to release the captives here. Every last one of them."

"Did you not hear me when I said how unpredictable they are? Certainly, your hearing is better than it used to be."

"It is, but unpredictable is just what we need right now."

The mighty footsteps we had heard in the videos echoed softly into the room as we talked, and they were getting louder. The rest of the group looked around.

A mammoth figure soon stepped from the shadows—an oversized beast with muscles twice the size of the biggest bodybuilder. It was the one Dr. Kepler referred to as Goliath, and it was at least 8-foot tall. Its neck was oversized, even for the creature's stature. Its skin was thick and leathery skin like an elephant; and it cracked at all its joints. The mammoth had a dark-eyed, thousand-yard stare that made mine look friendly.

I thought about hitting it, but it had a massive

jawline. It would have been a waste of time. I raised my weapon.

"We call these ones Bashers," said Dr. Kepler, "and I guess we could all use some unpredictability right now."

"Stand down," I said.

"What?" asked Elias.

"Lower your weapons."

"Are you out of your—"

"I said lower your weapons."

The others cut each other confused looks for a moment and lowered their weapons. I understood their hesitation. I knew Dr. Kepler was not a friend but, mentally and physically, I knew we needed to get out of The Tower with the changes going on inside me. Why Dr. Kepler wanted to leave and was okay burning the place to the ground was none of my concern. Enemy of my enemy... Besides, I still planned on killing him once we were out of that place, and he presented me with a cure.

We left the same way we entered as Dr. Kepler retrieved a silver briefcase from one of the tabletops in the room.

"What's that?" I stopped to ask.

"The LS-8 Virus," answered Dr. Kepler. "It is going to cure the world of its diseases."

"Can what you did to me be reversed?"

"It could," answered Dr. Kepler, "but why would one want to reverse progression? You are perfect now."

"Reverse it."

"Not now." Dr. Kepler shook his haed. "You will

need what you have to make it out of here alive. As stated, you're perfect."

"When we get out of here, I'm going to perfectly kill you if you don't hand over a cure."

"I will have it for you when the time comes."

I moved out the door.

"Archer," said Dr. Kepler.

I stopped but did not turn back. "Yes."

"I'm going to free the rest of the LS subjects. Every last one. I suggest you hurry."

I walked out. It was an odd sensation to have Dr. Kepler and the Basher on my six before parting ways. He did not control me like the other creatures in The Tower, but I could feel his pull. Something inside me, a small part of whatever I was becoming, was connected to him in ways I could not explain—like the way a newborn kitten knows to suckle its mother's teet without having to learn it.

38-2
THE BEGINNING OF CHAOS

We ran through the halls with creatures soon to descend upon The Tower. A soldier rounded the corner in front of us and drew his weapon.

POP-POP.

He should have been faster. A center mass double-tap from the pistol in my uniform came swifter than he could get a good bead on me. Two more soldiers followed shortly after. Elias sprayed his automatic weapon. An untrained wildfire of lead dropped one of them as the other fighters ducked for cover.

The remaining soldier opened fire. We sidestepped for cover, and he kept firing past us. He was not shooting at us. Something was more concerning than we were.

We looked to our six. Two of the first types of creatures we fought—a Jumper and one of the more human-like things that emerged from the smoked-glass pods—was running after us, which meant it was running towards him. They were faster than us and growing near, but the larger one took a shot in the head from the soldier and almost passed me as it slid to a stop on its stomach. The second was wounded but kept rushing.

"Move out," I called to the group. "The door at the end of the hall to the left."

Kat was out front and way ahead of everyone else in the long corridor. Draven and Anthony were behind her. Elias and I were pulling up the rear.

The soldier reloaded his rifle and paid us no attention when we passed him with the creature gaining behind us. It slammed into the soldier just as he locked in another magazine, tackling him to a slide at our right.

We could hear the fallen soldier's screams and helpless gunshots, but we never looked back.

Less than 30-meters later, a scientist was slammed halfway into the hallway through a glass window at our right. A Mimic was on her. Elias emptied his assault rifle into a window at another one of Dr. Kepler's creations until it dropped. Not sure which type of weapons he was shooting, I paid no attention to the rifle he snagged.

Elias discarded his firearm. "I'm out."

Another soldier fell from a door at the left of the corridor and landed directly in front of me. One of the Jumpers was on him. I hurdled the attack, but my foot snagged the damn thing's lanky ass head and tripped me. The Jumper mounted the soldier and whacked him as I got up and rushed with the other fighters to escape.

I turned back and hit the creature with three rounds, firing quickly into its head before my magazine emptied. The beast fell off the soldier. It was dead.

I tossed the empty pistol to the floor as the dazed soldier sat up. He wobbled a bit and gave me a thankful nod as he fell to his back and attempted to sit up again, but it was the last thing he ever did—because another Jumper dropped onto his head and smashed it like a melon.

It stood over the dead soldier's body and replicated the man's sporadic screams released during the last attack.

Kat made it to the door. "In here."

Another Jumper from a door across the hall leaped onto Draven.

"Mothafucka." Anthony grabbed the tall Jumper in a chokehold from behind.

I ran to help, but something slammed into my back. It was another Jumper. The floor came quickly to my face when it landed on me. It was already ripping at my back, and we had not slid to a halt yet. I spun to my back and placed my knees into its chest to create some distance between us.

Elias wrestled it off me and bounced from side to side in the corridor as I stood to help. It was a tough fight. It was stronger than it looked.

The Jumper broke free from my little brother's body lock and spun to face him, but I grabbed it from behind with its arms pinned at its side tight enough it had trouble breathing. Elias hit the Jumper with several hard shots before it kicked him a few paces down the corridor onto his back. The creature and me fell and rose back up to the battle. It fought ferociously and was more brutal than the other Jumpers we had faced.

I buried my knuckles into it with blows that would have decimated a normal man upon the first contact, but it dropped down and knocked my feet out from under me, lurking my way on the ground like a crawling spider as I rose. Then it stood, but Elias hit it with a running push kick that sent it backward, off its feet, and 10-feet down the corridor.

"Come on." Elias pulled at my torn jumpsuit to help me up.

We raced a chasing Jumper's speed to the door. Kat and the others entered for safety and tried to close it behind us.

38-3
NEW MUTATIONS

The Jumper smashed into the door as we tried to shut it. Elias, Kat, and I were trying to get it shut enough to lock it, or at least to get the damn latch to click, but the creature's impacts were heavy. It had to be hurting itself. I hoped it was but all that mattered s that we eventually got the latch to click into place long enough to lock it.

We did not know what kind of room we were in until we turned from the door to look. It was a Gene Lab that I am sure was once intact. Pieces of glass, microscopes, and a toppled refrigerator, amongst other things, painted a picture of violence. Dr. Strogolev, the one from the video logs, had her feet propped against another door in the back of the lab and was holding it shut. Multiple creatures were ripping into other scientists in the backdrop. It was far from the sanctuary we had hoped.

"Help me," Dr. Strogolev cried without looking back.

She did not know it was us that had come into the lab. Doubt she cared. She was in a frantic state of mind.

"Please," she continued.

We had to help her to help ourselves, not that I gave a fuck if she lived or died. I only cared about the others in my group. They were my squad—my pride. No man left behind.

Kat grabbed a rifle from a dead soldier while Elias removed a pistol from the lower leg holster on the same body. He checked for ammo. It was empty.

"The upper pouches on the front of the vest," I said.

He pulled a magazine from the soldier's tactical vest and loaded it, pulling back the slide to chamber a round into its bore. "Thanks."

I stepped past Dr. Strogolev. "Let it go."

She moved from the base of the door, and it flew open. A bizarre creature I had yet to see snarled with dripping saliva. Its skin was moist and smoother than others we had encountered.

"Elias." I motioned towards whatever the hell it was.

He squared up and fired a single shot to the upper right portion of its forehead. Not a second later, it fell to the floor in stillness. Another odd-looking thing—short, fat, bald all over, grey, and not very mobile—was mauling a scientist who was already dead and did not know it yet. Her injuries were too severe to survive, much less make it out of The Tower, but I smashed it in the back of its head just the same. It died instantly.

I looked them over for a moment, knowing they were nothing more than failed experiments. They were brittle and weak, nothing like what General Shepherd and Dr. Kepler were trying to create.

I stepped from the room only to have a stout creature baring the first two's similarities blindside me from another room. It was heavy and drove me into a nearby wall, pinning me to it like a fly to flypaper. It was bigger than the last and a hell of a lot stronger. Meaner too. It tried to gouge my eyes as if it were a bear digging honey from a hive, but I bit off its ear as Elias fired a few shots from his pistol. The creature did not let up and stood firm against me.

"The fuck..." Elias emptied his entire magazine into it, but the slimy bastard still snubbed its nose to the thought of going down.

I growled in its face like a lion.

Elias was starting to panic; I could see it in the jerkiness of his movements. He began to move for the creature twice but stopped, and I could not get my feet under me for leverage.

"You going to do something or what?" I mumbled with its ear in my mouth.

Elias looked around for a second before throwing the empty pistol at it in desperation. It bounced off the thing's head and fell to the floor.

I nodded. "Thanks."

"Fuck me." He jumped on the creature's back and threw it in a tight chokehold. He squeezed for a moment before it let me go to fight with him, but Elias fell to his back and wrapped his legs around its body so it could not escape.

I moved in, straddled both of them, and pushed my thumbs through its eyes just as it passed out from the choke, then squeezed and pulled hard enough to remove the sinus portion of its face.

Elias let it go when dark blood rushed from the hole

in its face and over his chest, then stood up to look back down at the faceless creature. "Damn, Archer. What's up with you and gouging out eyes today? And did you bite that things ear off?"

I spit it to the floor.

"Dude…" Elias paused. "You're fucking scary, bro."

Maybe I was. At least to him. It probably was not the best time to tell him I was going to swallow it before he called me out.

A loud, metal-on-metal clank echoed from somewhere distant.

Elias looked over his shoulder and back to me. "Where's Kat?"

Four more clanks resounded throughout the lab. Elias moved towards the noise, only to pause when small ceiling pieces fell and bounced off him with dust. He looked up as a Mimic fell through the roof and toppled him.

Kat entered from another room in the back and bashed it in the head with a fire extinguisher, releasing another loud clank.

"Thanks," said Elias.

She dropped the extinguisher and staggered towards him with deep fingernail scratches on her neck and face. "Return the favor when you get a chance, yeah?"

"For sure."

She helped him up.

"At least we know where the clanking came from," continued Elias. "What happened to the rifle?"

"It was empty," said Kat.

"Why didn't you hit them with the rifle?"

"Does it matter right now? Where's Anthony and Draven?"

Elias looked around. "We saw them fighting with one of those things that killed Haley just before Archer was tackled in the hallway. They didn't make it in with you?"

Kat shook her head. "I thought they were with you."

"They weren't in the hallway when me and Archer started heading back this way. We barely made it in ourselves."

A moment of silence passed.

"Take me with you," said Dr. Strogolev. "Please."

I had forgotten she was there. I would not leave her for the worms. Last week I probably would have.

"Come on," I said, moving with Elias, Kat, and Dr. Ivana Strogolev to exit the room.

"Wait…" The doctor stopped. "My research."

She ran in the opposite direction we were heading, desperate to grab something from a nearby table. At least that is where she was heading. I should have left the bitch.

"There's no time," I said.

She gathered a few folders and USB drives. "Got it. Let's—"

The ceiling above her collapsed. Sections of heavy foundation fell from above, and Dr. Strogolev screamed out before being buried under rubble. I moved in to help, but another Jumper peeked its head through the hole in the roof and peered at me—screaming replications of Dr. Strogolev's cry while maintaining eye contact with me.

Kat took a step forward, but Elias stopped her. It was a good call. The Jumper landed directly on top of Dr. Strogolev and the wreckage.

"Help me." Her bones cracked as she screamed. "Please."

The Jumper pulled her head up until her neck broke and she was gone, maintaining its position as it taunted us. *"HHHelp… me… Pleeeease."*

"Archer," said Elias. "Let's go. It's all burning."

I backed away slowly with my eyes locked on the Jumper.

"Archer," continued Elias.

I turned, and we made our escape.

CHAPTER 39
SMOKE

I, ELIAS, AND Kat came to a set of working elevators. Smoke was emanating profusely from the crack in their doors. The Elevator halls smelled like a burning electrical fire, and sprinkler systems were working in full force.

Kat touched an elevator door and snatched her hand off, shaking it in pain. "Shit… That's hot."

"There's a backdraft waiting for you in there," I said.

Draven and Anthony rounded the corner and stopped when they saw us. Their tattered clothes were worse off than the last time we saw them. New blood spatters riddled their bodies amongst fresh wounds.

"Anthony…. Draven…" said Elias. "We thought you got killed or lost or something."

"Shit," said Anthony. "Almost did."

"Yeah," said Draven, "on both counts."

Elias's attention went to a firehose and ax on the wall encased in glass. He looked back at me and retracted his arm to elbow it. The glass shattered.

"I don't think you're going to need that, son," said General Shepherd.

Where the hell he came from, I do not know; but he had us dead to rights.

We looked his way. Four armed soldiers walked his six next to Captain Warwick, who was holding the silver briefcase Dr. Kepler was carrying earlier. The thought of whether one of them had killed Dr. Kepler or not crossed my mind as Elias reached for the ax.

"He touches that ax," said General Shepherd, "shoot him."

"Yes, sir," said Captain Warwick.

The soldiers were at the ready and waiting to pull the trigger. Elias stopped. I knew he would. He was not that stupid.

General Shepherd eyed me proudly for a moment as the sprinkler system soaked us further. "Well, well. Look at you. Popped you with LS-8, didn't he? Shady little prick. Never trust a fuck-tard that breathes through air sacks in the back of his head. That's what I always say. You know he took it all? Every last bit of the good stuff." He paused to laugh. "At least we were able to get a nice surplus of LS-7 before he torched the place." He looked to the briefcase in Captain Warwick's possession, shaking his head. "It's that Goddamn LS-8 that I need, though. It's all the lean without the fat. Luckily, I have you. My personal gene donor. So, let's get moving. It's going to be getting a little hot in here shortly."

Soldiers corralled us at gunpoint and pushed us to the head of the group before forcing us to walk. We came to a set of double doors. Someone had snatched the card scanners at their sides from their positions on the wall. Sparks flew from it at random to stench up the air as General Shepherd gave Captain Warwick a nod to proceed.

"Yes, sir." Captain Warwick eased the door open with the stock of his rifle and peeked inside. "Looks like hell in there, sir."

"Details, Captain Warwick," said General Shepherd. "Details. What do you see?"

Captain Warwick looked through the cracked door again. I could not get much information from where I was standing, but I could see several bodies. They were overrunning The Tower.

Captain Warwick grinned. "I see dead people."

I looked into the large window running some fifteen feet down the hallway. It was a hybrid operating room of some kind. Lights flickered on and off inside it with infrequency to feed the hallway around us with wavering patterns as we entered.

39-2
THE CRACK OF GLASS

Tension was high. Our steps were slow and light. Captain Warwick investigated the glass at our right in search of something as we walked. One of the creatures was going through the cabinets, and glass doors entering the lab had been broken out.

Captain Warwick dropped for cover when he saw a creature. We all did, soldiers and captives alike. I am sure the creature heard us. I knew it was scanning in search of something to kill. I could feel it.

General Shepherd peeked in, waited a few seconds, and motioned everyone to move forward, but one of his goons moved too quickly and without paying attention to his surroundings. Dumb fuck stepped on a single piece of glass. It snapped.

I heard the creature spin and take a few erratic steps. We remained still and out of sight. None of us knew there were three other beasts in the wait.

An oversized Jumper stood tall. General Shepherd, his goons, and the rest of us were equally on our toes. We held our breath and braced ourselves for madness.

Captain Warwick placed the briefcase on the floor next to him, looked towards General Shepherd, and popped his head up for a quick peek. His eyes widened when the creature grabbed his head and snatched him into the lab.

The other creatures were upon him before he could react, and a chaotic shooting gallery followed when they hit the ground. Stray bullets flew in all directions. Anthony was hit and dropped immediately.

"Anthony!" Draven rushed to his side, but the bullet had removed a chunk of his skull. "Mother fuckers!" He stood looking for a weapon.

Elias was attacked along with the soldiers, but he was a tough hombre. He locked up with the creature that grabbed him, and they tumbled over the windowsill into the lab.

"Draven…" I turned to Kat. "Come on."

I grabbed her and dove through the windowsill, following Elias.

39-3
LAB FIGHT

We landed recklessly into the lab as Draven grabbed a rifle off one of the dead soldiers. He fired at both the soldiers and the creatures without priority, killing two of the creatures and managing to tag Captain Warwick before being shot dead himself.

"No," screamed Kat.

I grabbed the creature on Elias and rammed it into a large cabinet with a force I did not have just a few hours ago. It turns out I was still getting stronger. I shredded the Jumper with violently technical claw strikes. It did somehow manage to fight back. It, like the last, was tougher than other Jumpers we had encountered. They were getting more robust as well.

Elias was disoriented when he rose to his feet and in severe pain. Kat helped him up.

General Shepherd was on the other side of the glass firing his rifle at a larger creature: a younger, smaller Basher. He fired until his magazine ran dry and discarded it to reload, but the creature rushed him. It was met with a rifle butt to the face that knocked it back a few steps, but the beast advanced again. General Shepherd swung the rifle by its barrel and cracked it with a powerful shot to the skull. Its head whipped to the side and back to General Shepherd. He swung again, connecting even harder, and it fell long enough for him to retrieve the pistol at his waist.

TAT-TAT-TAT.

General Shepherd was speared to the ground by another monster and left to hold it at bay with his feet while popping off rounds.

TAT-TAT-TAT.

A few more rounds went into the beast before it died on top of him.

Flames were invading various areas of the Lab and hallway. Smoke was bellowing hard, and Elias was still out of it. Another creature approached to see me. I wasted no time locking up with it in an unpleasant dance to an unheard death-metal anthem: *Lamb of God – Walk with me in hell*, if I had to guess.

I slammed it into the corner of the table. "Get Elias out of here." Then it latched onto my leg.

Kat helped Elias exit to the Hallway as I flipped the creature onto its back and straddled it, biting at its throat and shaking my head like a lock-jawed pit bull. I could taste its nasty blood filling my mouth as I ripped my head up and took a piece of the creature with me. Only I did not find it as nasty as d expected.

Blood ran down my face and chin before dripping onto my chest in a slowly satisfying run. I spit the flesh out and swallowed what was in my mouth—my secret.

General Shepherd threw up in his mouth and swallowed. "Now that's just nasty."

I popped back up with my claws spread and showing my teeth, then I charged General Shepherd as he fired his pistol. He managed to land a few rounds into my chest. It hurt. It burned but only enough to drop me to a knee.

He must have seen the hate surging from my golden eyes as I rose again. I thought he would take off running, but the soldier in him fired a round into my thigh. I went down.

"Who do you think you're fucking with, soldier?" asked General Shepherd. "This is my tower."

He stepped forward and caught me in the face with a strong knee as I held the bleeding hole in my thigh. It knocked me backward and to the ground again. I thought that was going to be it, but he lifted his leg high over my head and dropped it to my chest like an ax. I winced but did not want to show him the pain I was feeling, and I did not have to. He knew there was hot lead burning in my chest cavity under his boot.

"I made you everything that you are," said General Shepherd. "You're just an ungrateful little prick, Master Sergeant Kemp."

He stomped my thigh, the one he had just shot—another wince. I rolled to my stomach.

"We could have done this thing together," continued General Shepherd. "You and me. You're a soldier, a killer. Always have been. Always will be."

I inched up to all fours as he struck me in the back of the head with his pistol, but I maintained my prowess as he pointed it to the back of my head, obviously mistaking me for someone with fear in his heart, someone more human, or someone who gave a fuck.

"You're as good to me dead as you are alive," said General Shepherd. "Goodbye, Archer."

It was pissing me off. I muttered half words through a half growl.

"I did not hear that," said General Shepherd. "What'd you say?"

I rose to my knees with the gun still pointed at my head and repeated myself. "I'm a soldier and a killer. But that's not all. I'm also a brother and a father, and I'm getting home to my son."

I blocked the pistol with my left hand and ran my right through General Shepherd's chest as I shot up from the ground. His heartbeat but twice in my hand before I crushed it and pulled it from his chest. He was still alive for a moment. His eyes widened and fluttered before he dropped to his knees and fell facedown to the floor. Eye to eye, he died knowing who killed him.

I removed his heart and tossed it next to a carcass belonging to a man I once respected named Samuel Shephard. He was no longer a patriot in my eyes. He was a shrimp hoping to become a dictator.

I looked around to find myself alone and wondering where Elias and Kat were. My instincts said to get to them, but I had something I needed to do first. The bullet was still burning, and I could not think straight, not that I was clear-headed at that point.

I took a claw and jammed it into the bullet hole in my chest. It took a little fishing around before I retrieved the slug from the bloody cavity and let it fall at my feet. I watched it roll in a circle and tilted my head in unknown curiosity before exiting behind Elias and Kat.

CHAPTER 40

BEGINNING OF THE END

I EMERGED FROM THE lab.

Kat and Elias were engaged in battle with a large creature, another smaller Basher. It threw Elias into a wall. Kat attacked it, but it tossed her as well. She slid far down the hallway with her skin screeching across the floor before coming to a halt.

I placed my feet to the floor against a nearby wall and launched myself from it, blind-siding the creature. The impact knocked it to the ground. My claws were tearing at its flesh before I knew it; and I was ripping large portions of meat from its face.

It was as if my limbs were separate from me and acting on their own free will, and without my mind's guidance or permission.

The creature grabbed a random piece of debris and

flung it at me—fallen metal or something from the ceiling. I barely had time to dodge it. Damn thing must have been upset it missed, buried its fist a few inches into the concrete wall beside it afterward.

Kat dashed down the hallway with the ax in hand and leaped into the air, burring it deep into the creature's forehead. She stepped out of the thing's way as it fell back to where she was standing and looked at it for a moment. Its head was split in two.

I ran to my brother's side. He was still recovering from the impact and had been dazed a few times in recently passed scuffles. I am sure he was dizzy. He was not 100% yet. I helped him to his feet.

Kat rushed over to embrace him. "I got you."

"I'm okay," said Elias.

He was not okay. He was not badly hurt, not like Haley had been, but he was lying about being okay. None of us were safe. Heavy smoke and flames were rapidly invading the floor.

I retrieved the ax from the dead creature and tossed it to Elias. "Take this. Time to go."

40-2
THE THIRD FLOOR

I led Elias and Kat unknowingly into a smoky stairwell under heavy coughs until we came to a burning barricade. To its right rested a door with a number centered high above it. We could barely make it out through burning, watery eyes:

'3'

We took the exit. The fire was heavier there, but the smoke was thinner. At least we would not suffocate yet.

Air wrenched with burning rubber, concrete, and stenches of flesh from human and mutated sources. My heightened sense of smell trapped burning hair and blood particles and forced me to taste them. It was nasty in the nose like an infected wound's pus would be in your mouth.

It was getting harder to breathe to make things worse, and the hallway ahead was blocked by flames. They were spreading fast to the roof. Sections of the building were collapsing, and I could hear the structural integrity of the supporting foundation weakening around us.

"We're going to die," said Kat.

"This way." I grabbed her arm.

Elias followed as I led them from the fiery corridor, avoiding flames as much as possible. There were a lot of them on that floor. Maybe it was the one Dr. Kepler started the fire on? There was no way to know, but it was of no importance.

It was getting oven hot. We had to go somewhere but could not go up. Smoke rises. We would suffocate if we tried. Below… That is where we needed to go. We probably had 10 minutes or less to get under smoke and flames before burning to death or suffocating.

I opened the first door I came to on my left, we entered, and I closed it behind us. It had not caught fire yet and mostly was clear of smoke. We coughed for a minute before exiting the door on the opposite side of it.

The choice to enter it led us to another lab with specimen jars we neither cared nor had time to inspect. A door at the backside of it called our attention as it had in the last lab. We made our way to it and forged through a few random labs to find ourselves a dead end.

"Shit," said Elias.

I looked around in thought. We were in the first of a series of labs housing microscopes and white refrigerators. I could see at least four more labs like the one we were in through connecting observation windows. Their entrance doors all went into the corridor at our right, but they were engulfed with flames as far as I could see through separating windows.

I picked up a stool and threw it through the window connecting the lab we were into the next. Kat jumped. I should have warned her first.

"Come on," I said.

"To where?" asked Elias.

"To anywhere but here."

Elias cleared away lower portions of clinging glass with the ax and climbed through. My eyes went straight to the window across the lab. It was about to meet the same fate as the last.

I threw another stool and shattered it, repeating the process three more times until we reached the last connecting laboratory. Corridor flames beat the separating glass with lively dances of aggression in each. An interesting thought crossed my mind—*a few millimeters of sand fused with soda, lime, and other ingredients had been melted and cooled rapidly to form the clear, 3/32" thick glass panes separating us from death.*

I went for the door in the last laboratory. Thankfully, the observation window next to it shed light on a few things: #1—It led to a different section of The Tower. #2—a thin film of fire was running like water over the next corridor's ceiling. I would have opened it otherwise unprepared. The overhead sprinkler systems were not keeping up, most likely due to all the chemicals and compounds in the area used for their experiments.

"What are we waiting for?" asked Kat.

I grabbed the door handle and stopped with my hand on it, taking one last look at the flames flowing through the corridor's ceiling beyond it.

"Go," said Elias.

"Get to the other side of the lab and get down," I said.

"Why?"

"Just do it."

He studied me for a moment and pulled Kat to the opposing wall, where they lowered themselves. I turned back to the door, pulled it open, and ducked behind it for cover. Flames surged over my head and filled the ceiling. It took a second for them to settle, and it singed hair from my arm as it dissipated. Had I not been soaking wet from the sprinkler system, I would have been baked.

"Let's go," I said.

We exited and cut left under the flames. A busted wall

with a goliath-sized hole allowed us safe passage into a large storage area not yet in flames. A soldier discharged the remainder of his magazine into a Mimic. Three more cornered him when it clicked empty.

They approached him slowly and copied his movements before attacking in sync. They gave the soldier everything he deserved as he screamed for help that I was unwilling to give.

We continued until we came to a set of double doors with a sign over it:

'OUTER TOWER'

A retinal scanner near the doors were tore from their hinges, and they swung wide open.

"I don't know about this," said Kat.

"You got a better idea?" I asked.

"Let's go, Kat," urged Elias.

We moved through the parted doors to find ourselves in another staircase.

"At least it goes down," said Elias.

He moved in ahead of me. I was right behind Kat as she entered.

40-3
THE BEAM

Flames were spreading. The ventilation system was winding hard to keep up. Thankfully, smoke was not as thick on the second floor.

I took a few steps into a nearby door to make sure it was safe for the others. The room was smaller than I thought it would be and mostly empty. A few metal shelves with ammunition at our right, and nothing more was present.

"Come on," I said.

We entered. I made it all but five steps before a fiery beam fell from the ceiling and trapped me. My leg was pinned. Heat seared my flesh.

Elias was almost hit as well, but it just missed him. It grazed Kat on the way down but only left a scrape on her outer left shoulder.

I tried to move the beam, but it was too heavy. If I could not lift it, no one else was going to be able to.

"Just go," I said.

Elias placed the ax under the fallen beam and pried hard.

"Elias," I continued. "Leave me."

"When did you become such a drama queen?" asked Elias.

I repositioned for more leverage and pushed hard to help as he tried again. He almost had me free when a Jumper attacked him and knocked the ax from his grasp. It must have entered the room after the beam fell on me.

Elias fought back, but the latest Jumpers were just too strong for him in a one-on-one fight. It kicked him across the room, standing all tall and proud in front of him. I will never forget the slimy and thudding sound it made when its head came off, hit the floor, and rolled to rest at the bottom of my boot. Its body fell to reveal Kat standing behind it with the ax.

"Thanks," said Elias. "Can I have that back?"

Kat handed him the ax. "How many of these lanky things are there?"

She caught sight of the number on the wall:

'2nd FLOOR'

"We made it," she said. "Only one more floor."

Elias moved to the fiery beam on my leg and chopped aggressively where the beam met the floor.

"There's no time," I said. "Save yourselves. I need you to survive this, Elias."

"Shut up. We're not leaving you."

A few more powerful chops and the beam pinning my leg lifted at its center like a seesaw then crashed to the first floor and nearly took me with it.

Elias grabbed my hand before I was in the hole and helped me up.

"Thanks."

"No problem."

"You two ready?"

"Ready for what?" asked Kat.

I smiled and leaped through the hole to the ground floor.

CHAPTER 41

GOLIATH'S PLAYGROUND

IT WAS A hard landing from a tall ceiling into a big open area. The sign on the wall said it all:

'1st FLOOR'

We were almost out, but the fire had already reached the ground level. Areas of the ceiling were rolling with flames like water defying gravity. It was creaking under the building's weight and releasing hisses as expanding air escaped timbers.

The massive cargo hold we were in was the keeper to a door we had longed to see. A window with sunlight shining through it was at its center. Sixty more yards, and we would be free.

We took into a jog, but pieces of timber and concrete landed dead-ahead at our 12 o'clock and forced us to stop. I looked up. It was bad. Flames were weakening the foundation faster than we were escaping.

"Let's go," said Elias.

Freedom was ahead. We rushed towards it, but an angry obstruction stepped in our path.

I stopped. "Goliath."

An unknown explosion rocked The Tower. Sprinklers stopped releasing water, and ventilation fans ground to a halt. One way or another, the end was near.

Goliath's massive physique was all that stood between us and the exit. If we wanted to get to that door, we would have to go through the big son-of-a-bitch to do it, and it was going to be a long trip. He was by far the largest of the Bashers.

A horde of other creatures mixed with Jumpers, Mimics, and the large ones we first encountered approached to stop behind Goliath. They were not going to make getting out any more accessible.

We were cornered next to four dead Bashers piled in the far corner of the burning room. It was the only bright side of the situation: we did not have to worry about more Bashers. Goliath had taken care of that for us, and his face reflected the blows he took doing it.

The other mutations eased forward, ready to attack, but Goliath's powerful voice echoed a building he was king in.

"Stop," he said. "This is my kill."

The horde eased back. We had to get past Goliath, but the rest of the creatures were a problem, and the building creaked as if it could collapse at any moment. Even if we could beat the mammoth, the rest would attack. There were too many of them to fight through.

I motioned to the four dead Bashers. "Don't play well with others?"

"My tower," answered Goliath.

My stance changed, claws showed, and an undertone of a growl was released. "Let's get this over with."

Kat and Elias got ready as well. The ax tightened in Elias' hands when Goliath brought his massive fists up to a technical fighting stance.

"That's different," said Kat. "In fact, I'd say it sucks if you—"

I attacked before she finished her sentence. Elias and Kat were but a second behind me. Three on one, that was the only way.

Elias moved behind the beast and attempted to bury his ax into its back but only managed to make a deep slice in its hide. It barely bled. The beast was not happy about it.

Goliath spun around and backhanded Elias. It sent him sliding along the floor further than he had in the hallway. The hoard parted ways as my little brother slid through them. They started to move in when he came to a rest.

"Grrrr…" grunted Goliath.

The smaller hoard looked his way and backed off, allowing Elias to stand, stumble, fall, and stand again before moving back to the fray.

Kat and I were attacking relentlessly. We were quicker than Goliath, but our techniques barely made an impact. Hell, I was the only one doing any real damage.

Elias attacked Goliath with the ax again, catching the beast on the front side of its right ankle as it stepped. It bought me enough time to run up the monster's back, grab his neck from behind, and tear at its throat. Or, should I say, I tried to tear it out. I was only pulling away an inch of skin at a time. I could not penetrate deep enough to get through what felt like four inches of hide.

I was sweating. Kat and Elias were burning up. Steam filled the area as heat evaporated fallen water.

The room became brighter and glowed orange and yellow from newly emerging blazes. That is when I noticed the center beam going up in flames and the floor above it smoking heavily. The beam was weakening. The whole building was.

Kat must have felt the need to do some real damage because she kicked Goliath in the balls. I nearly laughed. Nearly, but it just pissed the gargantuan off. It flailed about with me on its back but lacked the flexibility to reach me.

"Ahhhhh!!!" Elias swung the ax at one of the beast's legs.

It penetrated deep and became lodged in his leg. Goliath tore it off at the handle, released a roar, and reached back for me until joints popped in its shoulder. I tried to hold on. I felt strong, but Goliath tossed me onto the damp floor at its feet like a wet washcloth.

The horde yelled and released haunting cheers for their massive comrade when he hit Kat in the chest. She flew across the room.

"Kat…" Elias ran to her aid.

She was barely conscious and gasping for air. Something inside her was broken—had to be.

"Let's make a break for it," shouted Elias.

I looked at the horde and hopeless situation. There was no way to escape them.

Goliath leaned over and hit me. I faded out for a few seconds.

41-2
A MOMENT OF BLISS

The beautiful, lush forest area with Spanish Moss-filled trees and vegetation in every direction came back into view.

I was kneeling beside my son, and he was talking about the lizard he failed to catch.

"That lizard's quick," said Christopher.

"The faster you move," I said, "the faster it runs."

41-3
BACK TO HELL

Goliath was standing over me laughing when I came back around.

"The faster you move," I said, "the faster it runs."

Goliath's head cocked curiously upon my statement as I looked towards the now heavily burning support beam at the room's center. It was splintering.

"Now, Elias!" I shouted. "Go!"

"Archer..." he said.

"I'm right behind you."

The horde heard me. They knew I was up to no good and looked at one another, ready to attack, but I was not in the mood. We were all about to die.

Kat found the strength to stand with Elias's aid. They rushed to The Tower's front door as I surged full force towards Goliath. He braced for the attack, but I made a last-second detour and hurled my shoulder into the room's burning center supporting beam.

The impact was heavy and dislocated my shoulder. I looked up. The beam did not fall, but a series of deep cracks had webbed up its sides. Fiery red kindling and debris fell around me like tiny falling stars to burn my skin. I picked up a larger piece of the wooden debris still on fire.

"Pathetic," said Goliath.

It turned its attention back to Elias and Kat, moving

to intercept them. That is, until a red-hot piece of burning debris bounced off its colossal head. Glowing red embers flew in all directions. I was leaning against the beam in laughter when Goliath turned back to face me. I had no idea what was so funny about it, but the half-gapped expression on its face was fucking priceless.

"When you said Pathetic," I asked, "were you talking to me, LS-7? You're nothing but a failed experiment. Think about it. That's why you look like a rotten banana a jackal shit on that sat in the sun for a few days before being run over twice by a fat kid on a tricycle."

I could no longer help it. I started laughing. It is funny how something so stupid can bring such amusement in times of distress.

Goliath rushed with hell's fury and evil intentions as I braced myself against the weakened beam and locked eyes with him. He brought his leg up to stomp my chest under full sprint. I saw it coming but never broke eye contact or tensed up. I knew we had won, and I was finally at peace. It did not matter what happened to me anymore. Kat and my little brother would be safe.

The impact was hellacious. It drove me through the support beam and collapsed the room one piece at a time—raining hell from above.

Goliath looked towards the ceiling. A fiery beam crashed onto his massive body as I looked up from my back. I could not breathe, nor could I move, but a slight smile was creeping over my face for Kat and Elias.

"No," said Goliath.

Fiery floors above caved in on me and the surrounding creatures. I laid immobilized, covered with only a portion of the debris Goliath was, and in excruciating pain, accepting my fate.

I knew I was about to die when a hand reached in for me, but it was not the hand of God. It was Elias, returning to save his bigger brother.

"Get up, Archer," he said. "No man left behind, right?"

I looked up at Elias. He was coughing in thickening smoke as he took my hand to pull me out. Shit did not feel good. I was hurt but glad to have my little brother on my side again. He all but carried me as we made a break for it through the falling debris. Flames and dying creatures flailed around us on fire. Some were already dead and crushed.

A few creatures watched but did not attack.

"No," continued Goliath. "My kill."

I turned back to see the beast battling his way out of the debris. We made our way to the exit coughing and passed through as he stood, but Goliath fell with a roar when he tried to take a step. His right shin was broken and folded under his weight.

CHAPTER 42
FREEDOM

WE WERE FEELING blindly around the door's frame by the time we exited. My eyes were killing me. Chemicals in the smoke enhanced its painful nature, but we made it out.

"I can't see," said Kat.

"Just keep running," said Elias.

They carried me what felt to be a good 70 meters from The Tower's base with our eyes burning and lungs choking for clean air.

The entire building collapsed behind us, and we hit the ground for cover. Debris shot around us, but we could not see it through blistering eyes and encasing clouds of black smoke.

I only know pieces of The Tower were flying about because I could hear the impacts around me. The ground shook with anger as the once-mighty building crumpled in upon itself. Small pieces of it tapped off my body before a larger chunk hit me in the side, breaking a few ribs.

I clutched my side as the shaking ground came to a stop. Much like in my last skirmish with the Taliban, I tried not to breathe; but you can only hold your breath for so long. I started coughing. Kat and Elias were somewhere hidden in the massive plume of smoke and coughing, but at least I knew they were alive.

The air took time to clear but not as long as it should have. A strong current was nudging it away. Nonetheless, we were almost asphyxiated by the time it did.

I rolled to my back and looked to my left. Elias and Kat were embraced in a light haze below thicker smoke finding its way from us. I watched them thinking about how good they were together. My heart smiled.

"I see you're still alive," said Elias. "You're welcome."

I snickered and clutched my ribs to stand. The winds were strong, nearly to tropical storm levels. Warm as if blowing fresh off a damp desert.

Kat stood and stumbled towards the fallen tower with a final bout of coughing. Elias ran to her side, silhouetted by a burning building once holding us prisoner to dark advancements. The remaining fires lit a dusky sky to assist a rising sun. We sat and watched it burn for a moment in an unspoken victory dance.

We were free, and though the others were no longer with us, it was a triumph.

Elias looked over his shoulder and cut me a smile,

but it would only stay a second. Something had his attention.

He froze. "Archer…"

"What is it?" I asked.

Kat turned to face me. "Oh my god. Where are we?"

I turned a one-eighty to see what was behind me to wish I had not. It was spellbinding—transportation into impossibility. All were speechless.

We were at the top of a monstrous plateau-like peak with vertically steep sides. Densely covered vegetation lined everything within eyesight for as far as we could see. There was one hundred yards of ground between its edge and the base of the fallen tower. We could have run off it blinded by smoke if we had not dropped 15 yards from it when the building came down.

A large blue bird with a purple-tipped wingspan over 14 feet flew high over strange treetops with smaller babies the size of hawks tailing it.

I recognized nothing. None of us did. It was a rainbow of nature, wildlife, flora, and fauna too ridiculously different to imagine.

Kat and Elias walked towards the cliff's edge and stopped. I eased behind them.

"I don't…" Kat paused. "I don't think we're where we thought we were."

"I don't think we're anywhere," said Elias.

At the far left of the horizon, a glacier defied steaming temperatures and bled down a mountaintop, cascading into a waterfall of staggering height to mist its surroundings. Five-thousand feet of falling water was disappearing into yellow and red-tinted treetops in the distance. We were lost in a world unknown.

THE TOWER

Reviews help authors gain momentum and increase popularity. Feel free to leave a review for The Tower. You can also check out the author/s currently released and upcoming novels here:

www.crbuchanan.com